I0823434

THERE WAS A TIME FOR SUCH A WORD

HARPERVIA
An Imprint of HarperCollinsPublishers

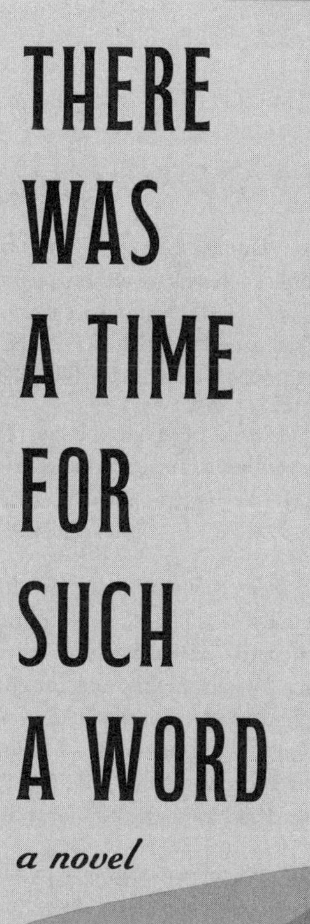

THERE WAS A TIME FOR SUCH A WORD

a novel

GIANNI SOLLA

Translated from the Italian by Richard Dixon

HarperCollins books may be purchased for educational, business, or sales promotional use. For information, please email the Special Markets Department at SPsales@harpercollins.com.

harpercollins.com

Originally published as *Il ladro di quaderni* in Italy in 2023 by Giulio Einaudi Editore.

FIRST HARPERVIA EDITION PUBLISHED IN 2025

Designed by Yvonne Chan
Title page art © Shutterstock; from Unsplash, The Metropolitan Museum of Art, The Library of Congress, The Art Institute of Chicago

Library of Congress Cataloging-in-Publication Data has been applied for.

ISBN 978-0-06-333616-2

25 26 27 28 29 LBC 5 4 3 2 1

To Titti and Dario

CONTENTS

Part One

THE PIG KEEPER

Tora e Piccilli (Caserta), 1942

In Tora they knew me as the pig keeper, the only son of Tommaso Raffaele Fortunato Buonasorte (nicknamed Furtunà), an illiterate, weak-lunged mushroom hunter, owner of fifteen pigs, and member of the Caserta branch of the Fascist Party.

We were country folk, knew all about the soil and animals but nothing about people. My father would say there was no point going to school—one pig plus another pig makes two pigs, and once you know that you can work out the more difficult stuff.

"If you know how small things work, then you'll understand the big ones," he would say as he mixed meal and bran in the metal bucket to feed the animals that waited impatiently.

"Yes," I'd reply, even if it wasn't true, since nobody in the village had more than forty pigs or more than forty goats, and you couldn't imagine the size of the world simply by knowing that one pig plus one pig makes two pigs.

Our surname is Buonasorte, which means "good fortune." The old folks who spent their days sitting in the village square used to say that words contained the truth or its opposite. Looking at the story of my own family, starting from my father's parents, who worked in the quarry at Maddaloni, both killed in the December explosion, and ending with me, born with a crippled right leg, it's not difficult to work out which way to interpret our surname.

We sold our pigs at the market, or my father would slaughter them in the yard in front of the sty. For each of them, I could remember who their parents were and who their brothers and sisters were. I could go back five years and trace the two main lines of ancestry from which each one came. Each pig passed something down to their offspring, except for Nero, who seemed to have been born from the oak trees in the woods. Once I dreamed of the wooden trunk opening and the old oak tree groaning like cows did. Nero was wild, ferocious, untamable. He was the most dangerous animal in the district, and my father couldn't wait to sell or slaughter him. He was the only one I was afraid of, and the only being on this earth I wanted to resemble.

MY FATHER APPEARED AT THE PIGSTY THAT DAY AROUND eleven. He'd been to the village to get medicine for my sister Rosetta, who'd been coughing all night. I'd heard her from the other side of the wall; she seemed to have a gaping hole in her chest. "It will go, it will go," my mother kept saying, but it didn't.

Rosetta had bronchitis for the second year running, and we'd heard that twenty children in Naples had already died of whooping cough. My mother laid the image of the Madonna of Pompei on Rosetta's chest and told us to make the sign of the cross. My father waited ten minutes to see whether the Madonna's intercession might save the money for Dr. Scognamiglio, then at three in the morning he set out for the village.

"It will pass, Rosetta, it will pass. Don't you worry. The doctor's coming. He'll tell us what you have to take, and if he's no help then the Madonna's sure to protect you."

Dr. Scognamiglio put aside the image of the Madonna of Pompei that my mother had meanwhile slipped beneath Rosetta's undershirt and asked her to open her mouth. Then he felt the bones of her arms.

I noticed the doctor's gaze as he entered the house. He had the same expression after he had examined Rosetta's throat.

He handed my father a note with the name of the medicine to buy. My father tried to read it, stumbled and stuttered over the letters, then passed it to my mother.

Between one cough and another, Rosetta was the only one able to read it.

"Well done," said the doctor, though what he meant was that the one person in that house who could read the name of a medicine might die that night.

"You don't need to read it. Just go to the pharmacist and hand him the note," the doctor explained as he put the stethoscope back in its leather bag.

Once Scognamiglio was past the two-headed tree that grew in front of our door, my mother and father opened the drawer to count out the money. I went to sleep picturing the banknotes on the table and not knowing whether I would see my sister again the next day.

"WATER FOR THE ANIMALS?" WAS THE FIRST THING MY father asked on his return from the village.

"I've changed it."

He looked at the trough.

"And you think this has been changed?"

It was teeming with flies.

I kept my eyes low.

"It's the first thing you need to learn, and don't you forget it. If the animals die, we die too."

He spoke calmly at first, then kicked over the bucket, spilling the water that was left in the bottom. The patch of water spread over the ground, and a tiny stream trickled toward my feet.

I'd have preferred it for once if he'd thrashed me like he thrashed the animals, to let me know he valued me as much as them.

"Move yourself. Get water for the animals."

The animals were aware of something, and Nero began to get agitated. My father grabbed my shirt by the neck and lifted my head so that I would look him in the eye.

"These pigs are more Christian than you and me together. Do that once more and you'll see what will happen to you."

He was right.

At that moment Nero charged forward and struck the wooden slats of the fence with his wild, muscular animal head. My father took one step back, letting me go. It was a violent blow. The wood bowed, and a few splinters remained buried in Nero's head. If pigs had stronger teeth, we'd have reason to be more frightened of them than of wolves.

"He's gone mad, this piece of shit," my father said.

Nero had defended me.

My father took the rake and went up to the fence.

"Wicked bastard," he shouted, beating him across his back. I thought he was going to do him harm.

"Stop," I shouted.

Nero fled to the opposite corner. My father didn't go inside the pen since Nero could knock you down with a headbutt.

"I'll kill you. You're the next one," my father kept muttering, using that dialect that connected our village's living and its dead, that single language spoken by men and animals when time began.

"I'll fetch the water," I said. "I won't do it again. It was my fault."

Those blows were meant for me, but he had found a way of making me suffer more.

My father had ambitions. I was his only son, and with me at his side he thought that he could create the small farm he dreamed of. But my body and my lack of interest in financial matters fell short of his expectations, and the boy who walked around the village dragging his leg had become a source of shame. My shorter leg had been a punishment more for him than for me. Maybe this was why he stared silently at the photos of fresh young army recruits in the newspapers.

Furtunà had his own way of keeping quiet, holding his chin with one hand and always working at something as if he were terrified of the emptiness. In the village he was known as a good person, but at home we dreaded his fits of anger. If he didn't take it out on me, then it was my mother. I never understood what drove him to believe in fascism with such vehemence.

IT TOOK NINE BUCKETS OF WATER IN ALL TO FILL THE water troughs, or eighteen half buckets, or thirty-six quarter ones. I scored notches in the aluminum with my knife. If the water stopped always where I had made the long notch, I knew exactly how many times I'd have to go to the waterspout. Once the troughs were half full, the animals would lean over to drink. The more they drank, the more my father was right. Nero alone decided not to give him satisfaction. He was the leader and would drink last, and only after my father had left.

"Now listen here," he said. "They're arriving in a few days, and we need to be careful."

"Who's arriving?"

"Hasn't anyone told you?"

I shook my head.

He picked up a stick from the ground and waved it in the air as if he were drawing something.

"It's not good they're sending them here."

"Who are they sending here?" I asked.

In fact I'd heard the old folks talking about it in the village square, keeping their voices low as they do with anything you're not supposed to say. They thought it wasn't good and kept asking, Why here? They must have had some inkling that it would affect everyone's lives. They said that a list had arrived from Rome with names written by Mussolini himself, but almost no one in the village could read, and Mussolini might have written anything on the list. The better informed said the list was in a drawer in the podesta's office, folded in four, and with a seal like all secret documents.

"They can't send them off to war, and they don't want to let them wander free," my father said, "so they're sending them here, as if we were not Italy. That's what I'll say at the next meeting. If they send one of them to us, I'll make him sleep and eat with the pigs."

The buckets filled to the last notch were heavy. I tried to spill as little water as possible along the way, even though my father's presence made me nervous. I could still feel that thrashing he'd given to Nero on my own skin.

"On the first thing they do wrong, I'll sell them off in pieces at the market," he said, and I wasn't sure whether he meant the pigs or the Jews who would be arriving in Tora e Piccilli in a few days.

he village festa saw the arrival of some actors. They were a rough bunch and toured remote places like ours, though we didn't know this. We listened and split our sides with laughter. We were an easy audience that laughed at anything, and the actors had only to tell the joke about the man who kept twitching and whistled every other word, and they were home and dry. There were people in the audience from Civitella and Tuoro and even my mother's relatives from Sessa Aurunca. It was cold that evening, and my aunt Tina wore a light cotton cardigan because it was the best clothing she had. She wanted to look smart. "Now she'll catch a cold and ruin the evening for us all," my father Furtunà said.

No one there had a wedding ring on their finger. They had donated them years before to the "Gold for the Fatherland" campaign. I always thought the real purpose of the campaign was not to stockpile precious metal but to send the message to Italians that they were married to fascism.

The flags fluttered in the breeze. The podesta climbed onto the stage and gave the Roman salute, and we did the same.

I had never heard Mussolini speak. I tried to imagine his voice from the photograph we kept on the kitchen wall. Furtunà had cut it out of a newspaper and pinned it next to the Sacred Heart of Jesus, so when we made the sign of the cross each morning, it was hard to tell which of the two was being worshipped. Mussolini stood in a field with his bare chest, flabby belly, and white cap and was bundling corn, while the holy face of Jesus that stared at us with his blue eyes and blond hair looked like one of the German soldiers we saw every so often in the village.

The podesta articulated every phrase, pausing in silence after each one. People said he sounded just like Mussolini. Some people gave the Roman salute; others shouted, "Long live the Duce!" Some said members of the Fascist hierarchy were there among the audience, watching for those who didn't applaud.

I was there for the actors. I had seen them the year before and remembered some of the lines by heart. They made us laugh just by the way they dressed. There was a man who played a woman, with a skirt, fake tits, lipstick, and a tight little hat with a flower on top. Now and then, as he spoke, he would lift his skirt, and even without seeing anything we'd burst out laughing. We couldn't help it. You'd feel the laughter coming from someplace far from your belly, and you could no longer keep hold of your body. The women blushed as they laughed. Even the priest, who watched the show from the front row, kept a hand over his face so as not to see but was careful to leave a gap between his fingers.

The actors made us laugh because they were telling the truth. They said things everyone knew but no one would say out loud. That was what the actors were for, to say things in front of the whole village. I laughed, imitating the other men.

Then someone came onstage dressed as a soldier. He pretended to be lost and asked which road to take to the war.

"Have you seen a battalion go past? I'm in no hurry. I could just as well stay here. They'll get me on their way back, then they can tell me how it went."

His uniform was at least two sizes too big and covered his hands when he raised his arms. It was his sad face that made us laugh. He had a special kind of bad luck that was funny. I liked him more than the others.

The next day in the pigsty I repeated the lines I remembered. I had recited them out loud on my way home and kept recalling them during the night. But even if the words were exact, they didn't work. I tried to improvise a joke about a woman who wore a light cardigan despite the cold.

"Look at me!" I said out loud.

The pigs turned, and with their eyes fixed on me, I could no longer speak.

That was my first audience.

IT WAS TERESA WHO EXPLAINED THE MEANING OF THE word *geography* during one of our afternoons together. But when I said, "This is the geography of my family," she replied, "You don't use it like that."

I thought of my father as the ditch full of lime at the far end of the woods, of my sister as the abandoned chapel that was said to be haunted by the soul of the old dead priest, of Nero as the scary old oak tree in which not even the birds would build their nest.

Rosetta went to primary school, was in the class of Signor Anastasi, the only teacher at Tora e Piccilli. I asked her to show me how to write a word. Sometimes she said she didn't know, and when she wanted to, she showed me by writing in the air with her finger. I followed the movement and imagined it on paper.

Furtunà would listen to our conversation in silence. Or he would say I should stop always asking her the same things. He would break off a piece of bread with his hands and chew noisily. In the kitchen, all you would hear were his teeth and my mother preparing the meal, chopping the onions and carrots.

The only letters I knew at first were in the names of the pigs. Gaba, Eba, and so on. For those that came after, I used names that I didn't know how to write: Grosso, Macchia, Cattivo, Nero. They were names that nature had chosen for them: Grosso was sturdy, Macchia was spotted, Cattivo was bad-tempered, and Nero was black.

My father said it was wrong to give a name to an animal that would then be sold or slaughtered. But I didn't agree.

I couldn't use Rosetta's notebooks to practice my writing, so I stole them when I went to the market, and even though I never really felt guilty, I never admitted it even to Teresa.

Don Aniello Panzer arrived from Naples and parked his truck at the end of the space beside the white wall full of holes where lizards hid. He was the first one there in the morning. He opened the front and side hatches, and when people started to arrive, he reeled off the chant that seemed like a prayer, listing his wares: a succession of words always in the same order. He obviously knew them by heart, and not everything he recited was in the truck. But those things he did have were cleaning products, broomsticks, umbrellas, thermal vests, cotton and woolen socks, men's underpants, pliers with rubber-covered handles, adjustable wrenches, tin snips, plumber's tow, springs, nails, candles, wax matches, and then other things that had been there for years and which no one wanted. Everything he showed you was German, he said. That's why they called him Panzer.

"Don Aniello, won't you try some of my *provola* cheese from Amalfi? It's German too," Don Michele would call out to tease him. Don Michele came from Salerno with a truckful of *provola* and *salame* and politely offered an olive to every passerby.

"What do you know? You live in the middle of nowhere," Don Aniello would reply. "I come all this way, and this is how you thank me. The Germans are another civilization altogether compared to us. They make things that work, not like the Italians or the Neapolitans."

The only items that interested me in Don Aniello Panzer's truck were those he had at the side hatch, the place on which he could keep less of an eye. There were boxes of black and colored pencils, set squares for technical drawing, metal and wooden compasses, little prayer books with guardian angels on the cover. I was looking for notebooks. Arranged in three piles, those with ruled pages, those with blank pages, and the others squared. When Don Aniello Panzer paused to chat with someone about her daughter's wedding trousseau, I would steal a notebook. I held my stomach in and slipped it under my belt. The cardboard cover would stick to my skin, and I had to remove it carefully when I got home, like gauze soaked in spirit that becomes a single thing with the scab, and you don't know which hurts more, the wound or the medication. It left a rectangle with its red border, the same size as the notebook.

The first thing I did was sniff them. The smell of new paper reminded me of a place in the woods where the wind carried the aroma of grass and mushrooms. Teresa told me that paper was made from trees, and I seemed to recognize every single trunk I had encountered. In the pigsty I pretended to write.

I drew pothooks, circles, dotted lines, then the letters that I knew, and finally I joined it all together to create something that resembled writing. I didn't know how to write but had created a language. When every page of the notebook was completely full of signs, I burned it in the bucket with some twigs from the woods. Then I went to get another notebook, which I kept hidden in the wool of the mattress, and began again.

ne afternoon I left the pigsty to visit Teresa. The sky had filled with clouds, and the smell of rain came from somewhere near. I walked through the woods following one of the tracks that had formed naturally.

"Teresa." I spoke her name quietly to myself, as if to remember the reason for the scratches to my arms from the thorns where the path narrowed. When you cross through woodland, it tries to coil itself around you and swallow you like a giant carnivorous plant.

"Teresa," I repeated.

I found her in her father's office on the first floor, where customers came for their receipts.

"If you've come for those bits of rope, return tomorrow. My father's over there."

She continued to study the accounts book in front of her as she spoke. She ran her fingers down the page, then paused to mark it with her pen.

"I haven't come for the ropes," I said.

"What do you want, then?" She stopped reading and turned toward me. I knew exactly how she moved her head.

In my personal geography, Teresa and the sea were alike, for I had only distant information about each of them. Everything I knew, I knew from what she had told me. She had told me about the Alps, about Pompeii and Herculaneum, about the Colosseum, the pyramids, the ocean. A part of her came from all these places; she seemed encapsulated in the things she liked, and maybe, like woodland paths, she needed to be discovered by joining together disparate fragments.

She told me about the sea because she and her family went each year to a house in Amalfi. There was a metal stairway that took them straight down to a beach of smooth, colored pebbles that shifted as they walked. Some of them she kept on the bookshelf in her room. They looked like glass. Teresa spent her time reading and sunbathing on that small beach. Her father came back to the village, to the ropeworks, while she, her mother, and her aunt stayed at Amalfi, sunbathing until the end of August, together with some other women who had rented the house next door. Teresa returned with her face tanned and white strap marks from her swimming costume. I went straightaway to visit her to see the strip of light skin that began at some indeterminate part of her chest and went round the back of her neck. I peered at that line through the freckles that emerged each summer from her suntan.

Before arriving, I washed my face in the stream and attempted to tidy my hair. The cold water tightened my skin, which felt smooth and clean. That was how I imagined hers to be. On the last stretch of road, the drops of water disappeared from my face, and that sensation evaporated.

She began to teach me to write the first letters of the alphabet. She told me how to hold the pen and how to keep between the lines. Writing was connected to the body, like carrying buckets of water or pushing the cart to market. I memorized her handwriting, which we used as an example. We had only just begun, but then she told me her father didn't approve. So we never mentioned it again. Each time her father saw me he asked about the pigs and about some pig fat I ought to bring him. He did it to remind me of my place and that certain laws could not be changed by anyone. I had to remember I was there thanks only to his daughter's charity: I was tolerated in their house because I was a cripple. There were other suitors in the village, though she never mentioned such matters to me. Then her father felt the hair on my forehead, still wet from the water from the stream.

"Dry yourself. Be careful. If you take ill, your father has only you."

I always hoped not to meet him.

I NEVER THOUGHT MUCH ABOUT WHETHER TERESA WAS pretty. Yes, she was, though maybe less attractive than other girls whom I imagined all the boys were after. She had dark hair and classic features, like those of her mother and her cousins. All the women of Tora e Piccilli had been born from a single woman, so all resembled each other. Yet hers was not a joyous beauty. Her face had a dramatic disposition; it had a melancholy, restless beauty.

"Read this," I said, handing her the leaflet. There were drawings with faces of men bordering on deformity. Large, curved noses, the upper part of the skull bigger than the rest. Enormous ears.

"Read it," I insisted.

Those drawings fascinated me, and at the same time they disturbed me.

"It's some kind of nonsense," she explained. "The words describe what is drawn. Here it says, 'Jews have a nose shaped like a six.'"

"What does it mean?"

"You know what a six is?"

I went to the desk where she was sitting and wrote the number *6* on a piece of paper. The circle was too large, and the upward stroke didn't follow the curve, but it was enough for what Teresa wanted to show.

She took the piece of paper and placed it on her nose, and the *6* became a big, curved nose.

"Do those coming here look like that?" I asked.

"That's impossible, don't be silly."

"That's what it says here."

"So you imagine everything printed on a piece of paper is true?"

"Have you ever seen one?"

"You remember Signor Horowitz? He came from Caserta to buy thirty-meter coils for his building sites. I was always the one who prepared his order. He knew English because he'd lived with his mother in London as a child, and each time he came he would teach me a new word. *Dog*, *water*, *sky*, *yellow*. I still remember them. He was Jewish. Everyone knew that."

"And what did Signor Onovis look like?"

"Horowitz."

"Horowis."

"As fat as my father, as bald as my mother's brother who lives in Salerno, with a big nose full of hairs like Don Franco, not as smelly as those who work here at the ropeworks, and generally ugly like all the men I know. Where did you get this leaflet?"

"My father brought it home."

"Can your father read?"

"Almost nothing. He says there's no point."

"This stuff doesn't interest me."

"Why do you think they're sending them here?"

"My father says they're forced labor. The government sends them here to work on the land."

"But why here?"

TERESA WAS A YEAR OLDER THAN ME. WHEN SHE TURNED her neck, you could see the movement of her muscles, as if the workings of her body were transparent. She was the best-educated person in Tora e Piccilli, along with Signor Anastasi, the primary school teacher. Whenever a letter arrived in the village, the farmers would go to her for two reasons: to get her to read it, and because they knew she'd tell no one about it. Teresa held the secrets of the poorest families of the village and found the right words to give news of births, deaths, marriages, and sudden illness. The farmers always thanked her with gifts of eggs or a piece of cheese, whether the news was good or bad. Once she came home with a goat after an inheritance had been announced.

Every afternoon she worked at her father's ropeworks. She kept the books in order and counted the goods that came in and went out. If she found workers stealing a length of rope to sell, she'd say nothing to her father and would alter the books. In that way, the books altered reality.

"My father steals more than his workers. It's as simple as that."

I didn't know much about what she did at school. She hardly spoke about her classmates. It seemed that she and I, for different reasons, had no friends.

I knew only a tiny part of her. The remainder was submerged like the city of Atlantis or like blocks of ice that float in the frozen sea and only a small part can be seen. It was she who had told me these things.

When other boys poked fun at me, she protected me like Nero had done with my father. They would grunt like pigs, or walk about on their hands and knees, or pretend to roll in the mud. They would imitate a limping pig. I felt a seething pain that turned to anger and would run after them. But even if it seemed I was moving at incredible speed, my leg only let me take short steps. My anger found no outlet, so I talked to myself or to the pigs.

I never understood why Teresa had chosen to side with me. I felt she was doing it not for me but because deep down she too hated the village. She loathed the families like hers that would gather outside the church on Sundays, hanging around the podesta so that everyone would know their beliefs—in the Church and in fascism, one God in heaven and one on earth.

Teresa was the only person to say that one day she would leave. And knowing her, I knew she meant it.

"Where will you go?" I asked.

Rome, Naples, Milan. Sometimes even Paris or London.

"They're our enemies," I replied.

"I have no enemies," she said.

As I watched her writing in the ledgers, I thought how we would both carry on our family businesses and would turn into our parents.

"I'll be the one to decide," she said.

Her hair had the smell of hemp from the ropes, and each

time I entered the ropeworks, I seemed to see her everywhere. But even in the woods I sensed her aroma as I walked past beech trees and wild geraniums.

Teresa lived on the floor above the factory, and her window overlooked the yard, which was also where the trucks loaded. Over the metal doorway, at the entrance to the building, were the words GLICINE ROPEWORKS. They were written in white letters on a green metal plate, like the writing on the grocery store in the village square. The first and last letters were larger than the others, under which was the design of a rope that joined the *G* and the *S*. Glicine was Teresa's family name. One day she explained that *glicine*, wisteria, was the name of a plant and also a color.

"Tell me what the color of wisteria is like."

"Colors can't be described. I'll have to show you."

"Tell me at least what color it's like."

She thought for a moment. "It's like a violet that's been kept two days in water."

Theirs was the only ropeworks around Tora e Piccilli. With ropes, Teresa said, people can tie themselves so they won't fall, or they can pull things, but a man at Caserta had used one of their ropes to hang himself. Things in themselves are never good or bad.

The ropes in the storeroom were arranged according to length: ten, twenty, thirty meters. The second criterion was thickness, and on that basis, you could work out what weight it would hold. The ropes were coiled around enormous reels that were the same shape as the cotton reels my mother kept in a tin box and used for mending Rosetta's stockings.

I don't know whether Teresa and I were friends. We were a boy and a girl, and at Tora e Piccilli, and in every other place I could imagine, boys and girls married and had children. It was never the role of a girl to protect a boy, and on the morning that she did, Teresa had decided what kind of relationship ours would be.

That Sunday we were in the yard outside the church. The only position I was allowed to play on a soccer field was goalkeeper, and I did it with all my heart. Everything depended on who was the center forward of the opposing team and whether he wanted to score a goal or whether he wanted to poke fun at me and take kicks against me. Renato, the pharmacist's son, kicked the ball along, then fixed one leg to the ground as if it were a crutch, and moved forward with the other. Everyone laughed and looked toward the goal. I laughed too because I didn't know what else to do and because I would have done anything to be one of them.

Teresa had been following what was going on. She and I had never spoken before then. Living in a village like Tora means you know everybody. Everyone knows whose son you are, whose grandson you are. They know who owned the land your father now cultivates, and who lived in your house before you did. We had never spoken before then, and we would never have done so if she hadn't been so deeply struck by the cruelty of the others. I saw her come onto the field. She had pulled a branch from the cherry tree by the church and advanced toward the center. No one noticed her. She was a skinny girl half the size of those she was approaching. In her hand she held a long, gnarled branch that rather resembled her. She went up to Renato and, once within striking distance, lashed out violently, whipping his bare legs. One single blow. I watched her arm summon all the strength it could, then release it.

That was the exact moment at which I started to think about Teresa. A mass of confused thoughts about her hair and those thin arms I would like to have held. Only later, when I started to visit her, did I come to recognize the movement. It was the same movement that the workers made in the ropeworks when they lined up the ropes on the storeroom floor. They would stretch out their arm and run a kind of wave along the rope. A whipping movement. She had repeated the oldest movement she knew, the one that was an innate part of her family. Teresa must have known that Renato wouldn't recover from the blow straightaway, or else he would have beaten her to death. There was blood all over the church ground. It was red, glistening, and resembled the blood painted over Jesus's hands on the statue that portrayed him on the cross.

Teresa then ran in my direction.

"You can't stay with them, you understand?" she shouted. "You must go straight back to your father!"

But I didn't want to be saved. My greatest desire was to be like the other boys in the village, and if it weren't for her obsession about saving people, maybe I would have succeeded.

"Get out of here," she shouted.

She put her hands on my chest, and after the first step I began to run as best I could.

During the night I dreamed of that touch. Her light pressure, her nervous arms that stretched out. She was trying to catch her breath. I could see her chest heaving. With the pressure of her hands on my chest I began to run. She did the same. We were side by side for just a few meters, then she ran ahead, and I watched her turn toward the village while I headed into the countryside.

Renato was taken to the hospital. His leg now had a mark that would stay with him forever.

An incident of such violence had never been seen at the church playground. Teresa's family made a donation, and the priest held a

Mass during which the saint was carried around the field. Teresa was put at the head of the small procession that followed the statue. She wore a veil that hung over her eyes. She held a candle in her left hand and had her right hand on her heart. When asked why she had done it, she made no mention of me. The procession beseeched the saint to purify the ground. The priest prayed, then knelt at the place where the blood had been spilled and remained silent for a moment. He had inconvenienced a saint for the sake of a boy who kept pigs. I followed the procession with the other villagers. I begged forgiveness from the statue, the Madonna, the podesta, Mussolini, the priest. I made the sign of the cross three times and recited half of the Angel of God with the words I could remember, inventing the others as I went along.

The following week I went to the ropeworks to thank her. I waited until my father had gone to the village, closed the pigsty door with the wooden pole, and took a shortcut through the woods. It was the first time I had taken that path, and it seemed as though I were sharing a secret with the trees.

"Why have you come?" she asked.

"I've come to thank you."

I spoke in Italian, not in the language we spoke in the village, which seemed debased by the animals and the land. I searched for words that would make a good impression.

"You stink," she said.

I took a corner of my shirt and lifted it to my nose.

"Maybe."

"Before thanking me, you need a wash."

She took me to the yard and made me wash my face, arms, and hands at the spout they used for rinsing the reels and the ropes. The water was cold.

"Get into the sun. That way you'll dry straightaway," she

said with a smile. "Don't you have any clean clothes apart from these?"

"These are what I wear in the pigsty."

"Not even those for Sundays or festas?"

"It's not Sunday today. Is this where you make the ropes?" I asked.

"That's what it says outside," she replied.

"I can't read."

"I've often told my father we could get rid of the sign. No one in the village can read. A picture of ropes would be quite enough." Then after a pause she said: "Sorry, I didn't want to offend you."

"That's all right. It's true."

"What do the pigs do all day?"

"They stay in their pens. Now and then we take them out. They wait."

"What do they wait for?"

"To be taken for slaughter or to the market."

"Do they know?"

"They cry. They know how much time has gone by."

Teresa let me see where they reeled the rope, the storehouse, and the office where her father worked. His desk was on a wooden platform. From there he could see the workers winding the thin strands around a wooden twister and the rope that gets longer and thicker with each turn. Teresa kept an account of the rope sold, materials bought, and time sheets for each worker. Sometimes she called me Davide, sometimes Buonasorte, as if I were two different people.

WHEN HER FATHER WASN'T THERE, TERESA WOULD ASK TO take the place of one of the workers. I had seen her do it myself.

"If your father found out, he would sack us," they would say. "We have families to think about."

"All this stuff about families. Everyone in the village has a family. It's all we have."

"You say that because it makes no difference to you. You don't think about us."

"I just want to help out, and I want to know how it's done."

"Your father would be furious. You know what he's like."

"He's always furious. Anyway, who says my temper is any better than my father's?"

She had learned to wind the ropes and could reel those that were thinner in diameter. It needed too much strength for the thirty-meter ropes. Her temper was no worse than her father's, and the workers knew it. She always liked going one step further in whatever she did, and it was thanks to her that on the feast of the Epiphany all the workers were given a basket with wine, cheese, and eggs.

In my afternoons spent at the ropeworks I learned about multiplication and division. I learned that Italy is shaped like a boot, which makes me smile even today. I learned that Tora e Piccilli are two tiny villages and that Caserta is not Italy's biggest city, like everyone said in the square or after they had been to see a marvelous doctor close to the royal palace there, and that there are other cities twice or three times the size. Maybe ten times.

Teresa was afraid of nothing. She wasn't even afraid of touching Nero. She said she had never seen an animal so big, and when Nero saw her approach the fence, he lowered his head.

"Don't touch him. He could attack," I said.

"I'm frightened, and therefore I have to touch him."

Teresa moved forward. Nero pulled back a few steps, but

there was no more space behind him. Stuck in the corner, he was nervous and afraid.

"Good boy, I'm not going to hurt you. If I have to come here, then we have to be friends."

She rested her hand on his head.

Nero calmed down.

"My father says, when the time comes, I can join the Young Fascists, but I don't want to," she said, stroking Nero's head. "When the time comes, as he says, I'll go off to my aunt in Rome."

"You have to take two buses to get to Rome."

She shrugged her shoulders. "It doesn't matter how many."

"And what will you do?" I asked.

"I'll find a job, carry on studying."

"You don't want to get married?" I asked.

"Like my mother, or like yours?"

he Jews arrived on the appointed day.

Legend has it that the devil walked through a place we call the forest, on the other side of the village, and left his footprints in red hot lava. They named that place Ciampate del Diavolo. The arrival of the Jews, people said, was the very reason why the devil had walked through our land so many years before. He had come to investigate and had decided this was the right place.

We knew nothing about the Jews, the way they lived, or the shape of their noses, but we were told they had to be hated. It was like receiving an enemy in our own house who was difficult to get rid of. The devil must have been cunning.

From the hill where I stood, it was easy to see what was happening along the road. Women and men, old and young, had gathered in the village square where the army truck would soon arrive. Some had brought chairs as people did when the saint was carried in procession or when unfamiliar singers came from Naples to be greeted as celebrities.

I had taken Nero out of the pen. My father didn't like it and kept warning me he was an animal not to be trusted. But with me, Nero had always been loyal. If he had escaped, there would have been no way of recapturing him. He would have gone deep into the woods, would have hidden somewhere, would have held sway over the other animals.

I tied a rope round his neck and gave it a tug every now and then, as a command. He could have dragged me away if he wished. Nero had given me his friendship, and this was why the other animals in the pen respected me.

When I saw the army truck climb to the ridge, I took Nero back to the pen and ran down to the square, which was the only space wide enough for the vehicle to maneuver and turn back. The picture of the Jew with his nose shaped like a six had kept me awake through the night and restless in my few moments of sleep.

I took the paths I knew, cutting through neighboring fields. Nothing like this had happened in the village since the arrival of a teacher from Viterbo—the first person we had seen from the north. He had come to stand in for Signor Anastasi after he'd had an accident. We had gathered in the square on that day too.

When I arrived, the whole village was waiting for the truck, and the question, the single, loud, precise, insistent question, repeated from mouth to mouth, prompting all kinds of fanciful answers, was Why had they sent them here? Why here, where we go to church every Sunday? Should we really carry the statue of the saint to Ciampate del Diavolo, as the old folks said? Should the whole village be blessed, as it was when Teresa injured the pharmacist's son? Should we make a new pact with the saint?

I went and sat on a low wall. The army truck appeared around the last bend. It looked like one of those giant fish Teresa had once told me about: a whale. A fish that could be as large as the church or three times the size of the pigsty. A whale ten times bigger than the army jeeps we sometimes saw in the village. The front part was rounded so that it slid gently through the breeze, while the line of windows was straight, and the sun glinted on the metal chassis.

"The whale," I said.

I was so rapt in thought that the word just came out. We knew nothing about fish or the sea, but everyone knew what a whale was. Marcello and Renato started laughing, and I felt like the idiot that nobody in the village wanted as a friend.

It was in that state of frustration that I saw Nicolas for the first time. I felt ashamed for blurting out the word *whale*, though I didn't yet know it was the only possible way of describing something gigantic that was about to happen to my life.

It was the moment that marked the before and the after, the inside and the outside.

NICOLAS WAS THE FIRST TO EMERGE IN THE MID-September sunlight, wearing a brown shirt and dark trousers. The sun shone brightly that day, and when its rays struck him full in the face, he shaded his eyes with his hand. I remember the slow movement of his arm, his fingers first tightly together, then parted to filter a more measured quantity of light, and his shirt, which hung over his broad smooth chest. I had never seen a more handsome boy. The notion seemed unacceptable for several reasons, each as compelling as the other: He was a boy, and I was fascinated by him; he was a Jew who had been interned by the Fascists, and the Fascists always knew what was best for us.

That was the first time I felt envy: a sin that would be followed inevitably by another, for certain sins are natural paths that drive you to committing others more heinous. This was what the priest had told us during catechism, but I had never imagined until that point of my life that it would be so pleasant. A few hours later, at night, I wondered whether my own feelings might have lodged in the hearts of all the other boys there. A sweet, devastating sensation. A rare commodity for anyone who spends the whole of his day with pigs, in a sty well away from the rest of the village.

I had still not imagined that it would hurt not being him.

The boy went and stood by the army truck. A man who looked like his father then climbed out. Another thirty or so followed, but my eyes were constantly searching for the boy who had climbed out first. He leaned against the vehicle, which must have been scorching hot, and looked at the old people, filthy children, fat women, emaciated dogs, all crowded into the square.

Only a few minutes had passed since his arrival, and the scene was already reversed. We were now the ones who were deformed, brutish, born in the wrong place.

The soldiers told them to line up in twos. The boy and the man he resembled ended up standing side by side. The guards ordered the group to move off. They picked up their suitcases and started walking. The procession marched off in military style toward Signora Ottavia's lodgings.

In the face of such an unexpected turn of events, wouldn't that boy have swapped his life for one of ours? We were Italians and Fascists. We went to church. The village's more able-bodied men had gone to war and were dead, and this kept us safe because we had done all that had been asked of us. But the image of the boy shading himself from the sun while trying to catch sight of as much as he could of the place, and with no idea how long he would be there, was like nothing I'd seen before.

Then I felt the blow. My body rose and crashed to the ground. Everyone turned toward me. They saw him before I did. My father had come to get me.

"Why are you here? Nero's pen was open. And if he's escaped?"

He had never beaten me before and had decided to do so in front of the whole village, the soldiers, and the Jews who had only just arrived.

I got up without saying a word. I looked across the square. The procession had left some time before and the boy would certainly not have seen me fall and get up again with my face red and blood trickling from my nose.

rom the moment I first saw the way he walked, I started to compare myself with him. Everything had become old, outmoded; every place inhospitable and unrecognizable. Nicolas was the living proof that everything Teresa had told me about cities buried under volcanic lava, or that enormous sea, the Mediterranean, whose name had the flavor of bread and earth, really did exist. He was the proof of a complex world impossible to imagine, a world that could only be contemplated in its beauty. I wanted to leave Tora.

I would later discover that Nicolas's essence was obscure, unknown even to himself, and that every attempt I made to understand him was a reduction to my own level. Nicolas did not control the power he possessed but was controlled by it.

I imagined for a moment what kind of life he led in Naples and saw a house filled with light, vacations by the sea, perhaps in a hotel with a terrace overlooking the beach, violin lessons, or long horse rides. I had borrowed this picture from Teresa's summers, from tales she told me about her classmates. I hadn't enough material to imagine a life such as the one that might have been his. First, for him, I built a picture of a large family sitting around a table at holiday time, and then I focused my thoughts and saw him alone with his mother, his father, and a girl as attractive as him, who must have been his sister. I could smell their clean clothes and the fresh polish on their shoes. Fine hardwood chairs, curtains in elegant fabric. But the truth was that I gained pleasure from guessing. I knew nothing about him nor about anyone else who didn't keep goats or rabbits.

Nicolas totally canceled out what I had seen on the handbills. I thought the Fascists must have distributed those pictures because they were afraid of anything that was not like them, afraid of the new world that was impossible to keep back and would sooner or later overwhelm them. I also thought our village was a species on the path to extinction, like those dinosaurs Teresa had told me about—animals that were capable only of devouring everything and, unlike smaller and apparently more fragile animals, had eventually vanished.

At home, I looked at myself in the only mirror we had, the one in my parents' bedroom. It was round, with a wooden frame. It had always been there. I had no idea where it might have come from. A wedding gift? What branch of the family had brought it? The only person to use it was my mother, on Sundays, before going to Mass. She combed her hair up from the back of her neck. Some part of her still retained the image of when she was young.

I went to the mirror, studied my face, and told myself there was no way I could ever be like him. To look at myself was the first thing Nicolas had made me do.

My parents had noticed the way I moved as soon as I began to walk. He'll learn, they said. If I had been a pig, my father would have known what to do with a defect like that. The Fascist's son couldn't go to war. Mussolini would have died of shame to see someone like me in his army. Our enemies would not have killed me: Worse, they would have laughed at me.

I stretched out my arm and touched my reflection in the mirror. Was I really me?

I looked taller and thinner than the previous time. My nose bone had grown stronger, and my father's face had started in some way to superimpose itself on mine. I pressed my ribs with the fingers of my right hand and found them strong. I tapped them with my fingertips and heard a dull thud, like when you bang a piece of wood to hear whether it's solid and how much weight it can support.

The boy I had seen climbing down from the truck was taller and slimmer than me. His broad, angular chest was thinner than mine. In a fight, I would have won. But that advantage was all I had.

I SPENT THE FIRST DAYS IN TOTAL ISOLATION, CONCENtrating on the animals. I rebuilt the wooden fencing that served to separate the animals that were bothering others. It seemed a good moment to do this job I had been putting off for months.

I gathered the wood by chopping dead trunks on the other side of the stream and carrying them by cart to the entrance, where I cut them up. Each piece of wood was different from the others, but the purpose didn't require precision. More important, each fence had to withstand the shoulder weight of the larger animals. I had to concentrate my energies, not to think, to talk as little as possible, to lift, carry, and nail, to tire myself. Suddenly this all seemed important.

My father came into the pigsty when the job was done. He gripped the first wooden slat and pulled it toward him with ever greater force. I watched the muscles of his arm tighten and his body turn rigid. The fence shook, but the structure withheld. I knew the force he had used was greater than that of any animal. He tested the weak points where the slats joined, and he pushed again elsewhere. He left the sty without saying a word. That was his way of saying it was all right.

Building pens for restless pigs was the second thing that Nicolas made me do.

arcello, Renato, and I had never been a gang. And if there had ever been one in Tora e Piccilli, the pharmacist's son would certainly not have wanted me to be part of it. But the Jews had brought us together. The presence of that body of outsiders had created an "us" and a "them," and our community of families, which had always fought over the disappearance of a few hens or over a piece of land, now had a common foe.

"The other villages refused to have them, so they've sent them here," Renato said. "We must do the same—if no one wants them, we don't want them either."

"No one's happy they've been sent here," Marcello agreed. "In the village, there's talk of nothing else. We've got to do something. It's our duty."

"Shouldn't our parents deal with it?" I asked.

"They don't want to take the risk," Renato replied. "They say it's up to us youngsters to do it, for the village and for the party."

"If we don't do something now, then more will arrive," Marcello said. "We've problems of our own. They should keep them in their own cities. We don't want them. People are buying quinine at the pharmacy because they reckon that they carry disease. True, Renato?"

Renato nodded in agreement.

The village had taken to the presence of Jews in quite the opposite way than I had. The light that had dazzled me had blinded everyone else.

"At night they sit outside gazing at the stars. It must be some part of their religion. I've seen them do it."

Renato picked up a stone and hurled it into the tall grass. We could hear the stems absorb the impact.

"What shall we do?" I asked.

"It's no good them coming here as if they're on vacation. They should stay shut up at home, like our families."

"It's no good," Marcello repeated.

"But what shall we do?" I asked again.

Renato's father had a pharmacy in the center of the village. They called him doctor, but he was a pharmacist. People from the surrounding villages came to buy medicines, and he ordered them from Capua, from Caserta, even from Naples if it was a serious case. The day after the delivery of an important medicine, he himself spoke about it in the square. He described the journey he'd had to make in his car after he'd received a telegram from the pharmacy in Naples, and all just to save the life of one of our fellow villagers. You're a saint, they said, kissing his hand. The Madonna must grant you another hundred years beyond your age. The pharmacy was small, the illnesses in our village were simple ones, and benedictions and quinine were generally enough to cure us.

"I've three iron bars that my father uses to thrash the dogs," Renato said. "They just need to understand we don't want them, that they'd better behave properly. It's best we let them know straightaway."

The talk of iron bars took me by surprise.

"And what do I have to do?" I asked.

"If you don't want to join us, just say," Renato said.

They waited for my answer. My fellow villagers were giving me the opportunity to be one of them, but there was the boy who had stepped out of the belly of the whale. Two different prospects. One of them I had always known, but not the other.

"I want to come," I said.

"You work with animals, you know what to do."

"I've never hit a pig."

"All animals need to be hit, otherwise they don't know who is master. Your father hits you. We all saw it. Maybe we should ask him."

"No, I'll come."

Sons are of the same blood as their fathers. Our destiny is written in that of our parents, and our children's is written in ours. We perpetuate the same miserable life in different bodies. If I'd had Teresa's strength, I'd have said that my father's life is not mine and I would turn out differently, though still his son. If I had said that I too wanted to get on a bus and leave, then I might have seen things in a different way.

"Just do what we do. When we start hitting them, you do the same, as hard as you can. There's nothing else to know."

"I'm not afraid," I said.

"I'm pleased to hear it. We'll be at your place at ten. They will be outside at that hour."

"How many are there?" I asked.

"That doesn't matter," Renato said. "We're stronger."

I spent the afternoon in the pigsty, building the outer fence. I hurled the hammer at the wooden slats. The wood softened at the point where the blow struck, and a slight dent appeared around the head of the nail. I began to hit harder. The structure I was building was becoming more complicated than necessary. But I had time, even though the burden of thoughts I was attempting to conceal needed more wood than I had expected. As I carried the timber about, splinters dug into the hard skin of my hands. I pulled them out, feeling no pain. I was turning more and more into my father. I stopped when it was dark and when my arms had lost all their energy.

At supper, no one spoke. Talking was a mark of disrespect toward my father, who had been working all day. Words were a sign of ingratitude. If we truly loved him, we had to let him eat in peace. When he was in a good mood, he would ask Rosetta to go and sit on his knee. Those were the times when we were all happy because our mother, whatever we said, would make no gesture to quieten us. She was the keeper of silence. She would communicate with heavy glances, coughs, or sighs or by shifting in her chair or pressing against the table. That was how Rosetta and I knew whether we could talk.

But the truth was that we never had anything to say. My mother sometimes had news about a forthcoming marriage or someone who had died, the only two events that brought any change in the village, two events that for me were perfectly alike. We received the news and mentally updated the village register of marriages and deaths. When it was a death, my mother would make the sign of the cross, we would follow, and with that gesture we were accompanying their soul to paradise. In the case of a marriage, my father would say, "That's their business," though it was nothing personal, just the point of view of a Fascist who believed firmly in the Fatherland and hardly at all in the family, which was its domestic substitute.

Other major topics of conversation were about animals at

a nearby farm that had given birth or had been put down due to some disease. These were things we always needed to know, especially if we found rashes on our animals.

"What's the matter, Davide?" my mother asked.

"Nothing," I replied.

My sister and I tried not to make too much noise as we ate, so as not to be told off. We had to wait for our saliva to soften the bread before we began to chew.

My father took his full glass of water and drank it down. Furtunà didn't drink wine. He rose each morning before dawn and was dependent on his body: The earth and animals were a religion for him. He genuinely loved his work. He didn't swear, didn't blaspheme, didn't smoke. I admired the care he took over what he did. At the village festa, he drank a glass of wine so as not to offend the other villagers, for he respected their work. He went to church because he was a good Christian like everyone in the village.

He turned to my sister.

"We must try to be careful. Don't go away from the house until this situation is sorted out."

My sister carried on chewing. She was nine, and her arms were darkened by the sun. She spent her time between school and the stream where she washed the laundry with my mother and Signora Isabella, one of our neighbors. Signora Isabella was almost one of the family and was the favorite topic of conversation between my mother and Rosetta.

"Someone will sort it out," I said.

Furtunà pushed his plate away as if he had suddenly lost his appetite. He spoke slowly, measuring his words. He was trying to contain his anger.

"You don't even know what you're talking about. You stick with the animals. With animals like you."

All I wanted was to get as close as I could to the boy I'd seen climbing from the truck. If I couldn't be his friend, then to be his worst enemy would be just as good.

I kept my eyes on the table and said, "And you stick with the animals too."

I don't know where those words came from.

This was something else the boy was making me do, though he didn't know it: Destroy what you have, start again from a new body, walk along a path you have never taken before.

I waited for the storm to break. I knew his anger and expected it to reach its peak in a matter of seconds. I counted to three, but it didn't happen. That evening, I escaped it.

"We'll sort it out. It's nothing to do with you. I'll stick with the animals, but I'm not ashamed of it like you. Other people aren't ashamed of the job they do. The ropemaker is no better than us just because he keeps his hands clean and wears better clothes. When evening comes, everyone's hungry, those who have money and those who don't. Those like you who are never happy, they're not fit for the country that the Duce has in mind."

Then he took a deep breath. His lungs didn't allow him to talk for long. That lack of breath had exempted him from the war, and his involvement in the local branch of the party was a form of compensation toward those who had gone off to the front.

I stood up.

"I'm going to sleep," I said.

WHAT I HAD SAID TO THE BOYS WASN'T TRUE. I WAS afraid. The night exaggerated everything. I was unsure about what we were planning to do, especially after what my father had said at supper, but I would never have backed out after I had given my word. I hoped the plan would fail, that no one would turn up, and in fact for a while I felt sure of it.

Instead, they arrived and whispered my name: "Davide."

I got out of bed and went outside.

"Take this," Renato said, handing me the iron bar. It was heavy and solid, smooth and cold. I'd been trying to imagine it ever since they had talked about it that afternoon.

Whatever we struck with those bars would be smashed to pieces.

"You're feeling up to it?" Renato asked me once again.

"Yes," I said.

"You know what we have to do?"

"Yes," I said again.

"If you're not sure, it's best you stay here."

"I'm sure."

"Then you'll show us."

I thought he was talking more to himself than to me, or that he hoped the whole thing would come to nothing through someone else's doing.

"Let's go," I said.

I was sure only of one thing: I wanted to get close to that boy. If desire isn't transformed into action, then it's no real desire.

We took the path down to the valley without exchanging a word. Renato, in front, had taken the role of leader. The same thing used to happen in the pigsty when the animals kept their distance from Nero because he was the biggest and had shown himself to be the most dangerous. He had attacked my father in front of the others, and this made him their effective leader.

Marcello's father worked at Teresa's ropeworks. They called him *'o sciacall*, the jackal, but for no specific reason, just because of some petty offense he had committed many years before. Most of the nicknames in the village came from the animal world: *cape 'e cuniglio*, rabbit head; *pier 'e gallin*, hen foot; *'o micione*, the tomcat. Nicknames were given to you as a child and would remain with you until death. More than marking some resemblance, it emphasized an affinity of spirit. Years later I discovered it was something akin to a primitive ritual.

"I need a piss," Renato said.

He stopped behind a tree, and we could hear a heavy stream. I thought it might be a good moment for someone to suggest we'd be better off going back home.

We paused for a moment, but no one spoke. It was our last chance, and none of us took it.

"Put these on," Renato said, handing us balaclavas. "Let's go."

I didn't like being ordered about, but that night I found it reassuring.

Signora Ottavia had lodgings where workers could sleep. They were men and women who came from Puglia, Calabria, or Molise for seasonal work. They spent their days in the fields and slept for the rest of the time, always tired and always short of money. They never came to the village, kept themselves to themselves. The Jews had been housed there.

We could hear voices. We squatted behind a hedge, then moved slowly toward the garden, where I saw him for the second time. There were three of us and two of them, sitting by what I discovered to be a telescope for looking at stars. That night, however, it seemed no more than a metal cylinder pointing toward the sky. I later learned it was his father's idea to bring that small telescope with them. They were taking turns to look. They seemed quiet and bored. Exactly as Renato had said: two people on vacation.

They gave no reaction when we attacked them. Renato took the old man, Marcello and I the boy. I had seen him and knew he was taller than us. He was thin, he could have fought back, could have resisted, or at least defended himself. Instead, nothing. Even the old man remained still. The three of us were ready for anything apart from this. It would have been easier if they had fought back. Only their hands, over which fear afforded no control, moved hurriedly to cover their faces through some age-old protective instinct. I moved in the same way that my father had done that day when he hit Nero, but without the same force, without the same determination. I saw my companion's blows land in places where they would have no effect, while my own were pathetic imitations of hatred.

When the boy lay motionless on the ground, Marcello and I stopped. Neither of us had had the courage to hit hard. We did little else than swear in our own dialect, which neither the boy nor the old man would have understood. Their words were also incomprehensible. A prayer in their own language, perhaps? The old man lay on his stomach, his head to one side. Renato had taken the same care as we had. The man turned in the direction of the boy as if to offer protection with his thoughts. There were pieces of telescope all about. Fragments of metal and glass stuck into the ground.

I'd have given anything to look inside, but Renato had smashed it to pieces.

Before we left, the boy whispered: "*Maiali.*" Pigs.

ake them to Ciampate ro Riàuru," Sabatino said.

He was sitting outside his shop. At his feet was a blind dog that found its way only with its nose and was always barking, as if it could see the devil in the darkness. But that day the dog was silent, squatting on the ground.

"Do you know how to get there?" he asked.

Beside him were two well-dressed women wearing hats, both with rucksacks on their backs. I had never seen people with such fair skin. They seemed very hot because they lifted their heads in search of air. I was nine at the time and was allowed to go and play in the square.

"To Ciampate del Diavolo?"

"They want to see it."

I looked at the two women. They were holding books and strange objects, including a contraption I later discovered to be a camera.

One of them came up to me and bent down. She looked into my eyes. It was the first time I had smelled a woman's perfume, on her clothes and in her hair.

"Will you take us? We'll give you a tip."

"A what?" I asked.

"He's deaf," Sabatino said.

The woman turned toward him. "Money," she said.

"What are you going to do there?" I asked.

"We want to take photographs and see how the rocks are made."

"The stones?"

"Yes. They're very old, and we'd like to study them."

"Study stones?"

"D'you want to go, or don't you?" Sabatino asked.

"Everything can be studied," the woman said.

"Let's go," I answered.

It wouldn't take long. They didn't know the place, whereas I had been there dozens of times. As soon as we started to move, the woman I had talked to—and later discovered to be the only one who spoke Italian—said, "Poor child," and then, turning to the other, "*Pauvre enfant.*"

When we arrived at the Ciampate, I went to sit on the rocks, which at that hour were scorching. The lizards had gathered in the hottest places. They scurried off when they heard our footsteps.

In addition to the camera, the two women had a pair of binoculars. I didn't know what they were. The one who didn't speak Italian had them around her neck, then held them and looked into the distance. The other meanwhile went up to the rocks, stared at them for a minute, then pressed her finger on a button on top of the camera, and I heard what sounded like the click of a spring.

They did pencil drawings and wrote something in a notebook with a black cover.

Then the woman returned and took some coins from the leather rucksack that had been on her shoulders until then. I opened my hand.

"Here, take it," she said.

I pointed at the other woman.

"I don't understand," she said.

I pointed to the binoculars the other woman had around her neck.

"I want to see inside."

"Into the binoculars?"

I nodded.

"Don't you want the money?"

"No."

"*Valeria, apporte-moi les jumelles.*"

"*Les jumelles*?"

"*Il veut regarder dans les jumelles.*"

The woman came toward me. Only then did I realize she had kept her distance, had remained suspicious throughout. She removed the binoculars and handed them to me. I put them to my eyes, and it took me a few moments to focus on the landscape. I saw roads across the fields that I didn't even know existed, and houses with red roofs, and patches of farmland.

I discovered that other places existed beyond Tora e Piccilli.

t was only during the night that I realized Nicolas had said it because he had found me out. No one else in Tora e Piccilli had that smell. He had recognized it, maybe he had once smelled it during an outing in the countryside.

Maiali. Pigs.

It was the first time that I heard his perfect Italian. A direct, precise language. Even Signor Anastasi shouted at the children in dialect when he was angry. He called them sheep, goats, but he said it in the language they all spoke, otherwise it wouldn't have been offensive, and the children would have started laughing.

The *m* of *maiali* rests on the *a*, and that short *i* is a run-up to the last letters.

Maiali.

I tried. I held back on the *m* and pronounced the *a* with my whole mouth.

It seemed like a new word. *Maiali* were no longer the animals I knew. I saw them from another point of view. I saw the difference between them and us. I saw their association with instinct and with the land. It was another sign of the influence

Nicolas would have on me—the influence of words. And from his mouth, even those words I had already heard came out quite differently, and sound and meaning became a single thing.

Maiali.

I took one of the notebooks I had stolen from Aniello Panzer. I rolled it up, put it to my eye, and pointed it to the sky. The paper cylinder separated the moon from the rest of my view. I could see its color, which seemed to have patches of white and yellow, and the light that reflected along the glossy paper walls of its cover seemed brilliant and dazzling.

WORD SPREAD AROUND THE VILLAGE THAT TWO JEWS had been beaten up during the night on Signora Ottavia's land. Certain rumors spread quickly, especially those dressed up as justice, since it is something that people always crave, and there's not a single man on earth who is not convinced he has been wronged. That's something I would soon learn.

News of the attack gladdened people's hearts. There's someone to protect us. The Duce has not forgotten us.

After I had fed the animals, I went to the village to take wood to Don Mariano.

I pushed the cart across the square and under the archway. The old part of the village began from that narrow street that climbed and twisted back and forth. Hidden past the inward turn were houses higher up, which gradually appeared to compensate for each step that grew steeper.

The weight of the logs I was transporting doubled at each turn. I was strong enough to make that journey twenty times a day, though the movement of my legs was awkward. The last bend took you to the Church of San Simeone. The gate to the entrance yard was kept open. On the left was the village tower, built with thousands of stone blocks of a color lighter than the rest of the village. There were two bells on top, one large and one small, and the clock below.

"Come here," said Don Mariano when he saw me. "Move yourself. Stop wasting time."

We passed along the central nave.

"Make the sign of the cross."

"I have the wood," I said.

"The only thing you always have is a ready excuse."

We went into the sacristy and from there into a small courtyard.

"Put it under cover, not like you did last time so that it gets wet when it rains."

"Here?" I asked, pointing.

"Further under. You're a good-for-nothing, not like that saint of a man, your father."

I unloaded the cart and began stacking the logs as he had told me. I made one pile and then, when it was too high, I began another one.

"Did you say your prayers this morning?" he asked.

"I never say them."

"What patience our village saint must have. Have you heard what happened?"

"No," I replied.

"And how could you know about it, always stuck with animals in the middle of the countryside? The Lord will take you under His protection. You live far away from temptation, a simple, fine young soul."

"I'm not a fine young soul," I said.

"The Lord has made you that way. He loves us all."

"In that case, He could have made me like everybody else," I said.

"But how can you say that? Everything is made in His likeness. That's not to say there's no meaning to it, even if you can't understand why."

"I thought He had made me like this in a moment of absent-mindedness, and instead He did it on purpose," I said.

"You just put the wood where I told you and stop chattering . . . We're in church . . . Show some respect."

People said Don Mariano was a woman in a man's body. The church, which he kept like a home, was a refuge from which he never left. Fascists made the sign of the cross when they entered and would never have dared to harm him within a few steps of the crucifix. Every now and then, people would make jokes about him in the village square: "Have you been to confession? And who confessed you, Don Mariano?" And they'd laugh, as if you could replace *confessed* with whatever verb you wished.

Don Mariano closed his eyes for a moment as if he were praying.

"We all know it wasn't right for them to send them here."

"Who are you talking about?" I asked, pretending not to understand.

"We're good people in this village. Wouldn't it be better to have kept them in Naples, a city so big? They could have found something for them to do. I know so little of the world. I have the word of God to keep me busy. They seem to be good people too, like us. I don't understand the differences."

"What's happened?"

"There are animals in this village, but not like the ones you keep. There are those who take pleasure in doing evil because life makes them bitter, and they gang up against one or two."

The words he spoke described me perfectly.

"Last night they attacked them."

"Who did?"

"No one knows. It could have been the whole village. Only wretched souls take it out on other wretched souls."

Now he was speaking for himself. He was the one who had been beaten in the middle of the night and felt those blows struck by all the wretched souls of the world.

"Why doesn't anyone want them?" I asked.

"We are good people, and there are certain things we cannot judge. We can only pray for them and for those who did it. It would have been better to send them somewhere else. They are city people. Sending them here was a mistake. I wouldn't like to say Mussolini was wrong, but maybe he could have chosen a bigger place where they wouldn't have been noticed. There are so few of us here."

"Are they dead?"

I don't know why I asked that.

"No, no. They called for Dr. Scognamiglio. He went to see them and treated them. They're fine."

"And who paid the doctor?"

"The doctor didn't want money. He apologized on behalf of the village."

"Is the wood all right like that?"

"Fine, fine, and before you leave, go and say a Hail Mary in church below the altar."

"Why, what sin have I committed?"

He motioned with his head to indicate the door that led from the yard into the sacristy.

"Move yourself, there before the altar."

There was no one in church. I felt the gaze of the statues,

of San Simeone on the left and Jesus pointing to his heart on the right. The pupils of their ceramic eyes seemed to follow me. Maybe they knew. I wondered why no one in the village had given my name. All it needed was the right question: Who could be so envious?

I started to pray, but the words, even though I said them quietly, so that I could hear them and let the Madonna hear them, kept being interrupted by my thoughts about the previous night. There was something else I couldn't get out of my mind: the bits of telescope. I still remembered looking through the binoculars of the French woman, the researcher. They were small, hardly sufficient to magnify an object just a few hundred meters away, yet they had astonished me. I imagined what it must be like to look at the stars.

I knelt and said a few words of apology in our dialect that seemed more genuine than the prayers we learned by heart.

"It was me, I won't do it again, don't make my pigs die, don't make my sister die. I won't do it again. Please, please let me look through a telescope."

I made the sign of the cross, looked at the statue of San Simeone to check we were agreed, and left the church with my head bowed.

e's called Nicolas," Teresa said.

"I've never heard the name," I replied.

"Nicolas. It's like Nicola, with an *s* at the end. There are many with that name in the village, like Signora Annunziata's nephew."

"Nicolàs," I tried.

"Nícolas," she repeated, emphasizing the first syllable. She pronounced the word in a single breath, while I stumbled on the final letters.

"Show me how it's written."

Teresa wrote it on an empty part of one of the account books she had in front of her. I watched the strokes form on the page as if they held the secret of his name or that bold manner in the way he walked. Or the reason why he hadn't defended himself during the attack.

"Is that how you write the *n*?" I asked.

"Yes. Look, if you add another arch, it becomes an *m*."

I kept seeing similarities between Nero and Nicolas: their strength, which was impetuous in one and restrained in the other; the elegance of the leader of the pack; and the beauty that made him different and superior.

I repeated it again, aloud.

"It's not a nice name. It sounds strange."

"It sounds strange because you've never heard it. It's like that, at first, with all new things. He spends his time with his father. They do small jobs in the fields, though they come from the city and know nothing about such things."

"He's here with his father?" I asked with apparent disinterest.

"They were brought here together. His father taught at a high school in Naples. Signora Ottavia told my father that he worked at a good school."

"Were they rich?"

"I don't know, but Signora Ottavia wouldn't have used such respectful words if they'd been poor. His father has set up a kind of school in the place where they're staying. Nobody must know, however. It's a secret school."

"Why secret?" I asked.

"Jews can't go to our schools, so his father is teaching Nicolas himself. He's treating him like one of his pupils."

"Why can't they go to school?"

"Schools now are only for Aryans."

"What are Aryans?"

"That's a strange question for the son of a Fascist. It's us."

"Me as well?"

"Everyone who lives here."

Teresa looked out of the window as if to confirm she was talking not just about Tora but about Caserta and Naples and every other place we'd heard about in Italy.

"Renato and Marcello too?"

Teresa smiled. "I reckon they're even more Aryan than us. They seem to be proud of what they are. I don't know, I can't explain very well."

"Are there Jews in the school where you go?" I asked.

"There were two girls. They weren't my friends, in the sense that we had never spoken. I saw them when we did gymnastics. They had soft, slim bodies. I always had the feeling they were lighter when they moved, though I've never said that to anyone. There are some things, when you say them, that make others think you're mad or strange, no?"

"Where are they now?"

"One of them managed to escape to America with her family. The other, we don't know where she is. It's not right what's going on."

"Who goes to the school his father runs, apart from Nicolas?"

"The nephew of one of Signora Ottavia's workers, and a shepherd."

"What shepherd?"

"I don't know him. He's old."

"What's he learning if he's old? To read and write?"

"He can read and write. He's learning mathematics."

"Numbers?"

"There are things more complicated than knowing how to count from one to ten. Mathematicians try to explain how the world and the universe function. Everything can be described through numbers. The sizes of circles in the trunks of oak and chestnut trees. The force with which water flows down a stream, the distance a stone will travel when you throw it, how far a dragonfly can go with a single flap of its wings. Numbers give sense to the world."

For a moment I felt tempted to tell her what we had done.

That I had gone there at night and hit the boy for no particular reason and that what I had done scared me and attracted me at the same time. Maybe I didn't want to keep on talking about him and his father's school. I had asked San Simeone for forgiveness, but I wasn't truly sorry because it was that state of confusion that had led me to act.

I wanted Teresa to know I could be just as dangerous as the animals in the woods, or as Nero. This was the idea I had formed about love.

At home I wrote out numbers from one to ten in a notebook. I began at the beginning of the line and ended when I reached ten, being careful how I arranged them on the page, as if I were contributing in some way to the truth of the world that Teresa had talked about. My feelings were confused, but I always kept the bounds of our friendship clearly in mind. Maybe it was just as her father said, that I was a good-for-nothing who turned up at their house with his wet face, taking advantage of his daughter's kindness. I was conscious of an invisible boundary, but I somehow had to overcome it.

I kept my hand still, with my wrist pressed against the sheet of paper. My hand moved awkwardly. It was more accustomed to carrying full buckets of animal feed. I stopped writing when there was no more space on each line.

Later I went to the pigsty, and on each pen I wrote a number, beginning with one, inscribing the wood with my pencil. I had to go over the wood many times until it softened to absorb the line. I reached eight. Eight pens. Two pigs for each pen, and Nero by himself in number five.

"This is your number, Nero. Number five. A nice number. You should be pleased."

I felt as if the numbers had brought order to the pigsty.

OVER THE NEXT FEW DAYS I FORGOT ALL ABOUT THE BOY and his father, about the secret school, about the mathematics that explained the circles in tree trunks, and about what we had done that night. The earth had its own times, and we followed them in accordance with age-old laws. I heard my father bargaining for the sale of two pigs with a man who had come from Caserta with an open truck. After he had sworn over the heads of us all that the animals had been fed on the best pig feed and kept clean to avoid parasites, the price was reached. I led the animals to the truck. Then I dug furrows in the vegetable patch for sowing peas, dividing the ground into exactly ten lines, ten straight paths that ended exactly where the stone track began. For several days my thoughts about Teresa were kept away.

During those October days there was still plenty of light, and it was still warm while the woods prepared themselves for a new fall and a new winter. Everything changed color and grew bleaker. Winter was the time when the woodland changed to protect itself from its worst enemy, the cold.

One day I saw my father talking to a man. He was some distance away, and I couldn't work out who he was. My father pointed toward me, they shook hands, and as the man walked off my father came to the pigsty.

"Who was it?" I asked.

"Mastronardo, from Signora Ottavia's estate."

"He wants firewood?"

"No. We've got to go and look at their fence. It was damaged in last year's rains. It needs mending and repainting."

"With all the Jews they have staying there, they have to ask us?"

"They all work in the fields, and anyway what is it to you? They pay us. It's work."

"We have to go now?"

"They're waiting for us."

Many able-bodied men were at war, and the only people left in the village were the elderly or women or those like us who couldn't go. For this reason, they often came asking us to do small repair jobs. We could nail, paint, and saw wood, and the people in the village used to pay us with eggs or potatoes or, if the job was more complicated, with a hen. Food was more important than money.

We set off with the barrow full of wood and tools. We would cut the perfect piece with the saw and would nail it where it was needed. I had already shown my skill in building hatches that slid or opened on hinges I had salvaged from derelict houses at the far end of the village.

We arrived at the very place where I'd carried out the attack with the other boys. When I saw it again, my heart began to thump. Several days had gone by and nobody now mentioned it, but I still felt my stomach quake.

"We'll start from here," my father said.

We worked all morning on the fence, then my father went back to our pigsty while I had to finish the painting. The smell of paint hurt my eyes, and I had the same burning feeling in my throat if I took a deep breath.

Mastronardo arrived a couple of hours later. He lived on the estate with his family and looked after all of it. He examined the job carefully, testing it with his hand to check how solidly it was done.

"That seems all right now. How long will it take to finish?"

I didn't know for sure. I looked at what remained.

"If you're in a hurry, get the Jews to do it," I said.

Mastronardo gave a sigh.

"That's no business of yours. Tell me how long it will take."

"Another half day," I answered quickly.

"It's getting late, come back tomorrow morning at seven."

I returned the following day, alone. It was hot. I took some nails and a few bits of wood in case Mastronardo wanted me to mend other parts. When I reached the fence, I found Nicolas. I hesitated before approaching. He was stretched out on the grass, his legs crossed, bare-chested, gazing at the sky. He had a gauze bandage on his chest, a wide dressing, and I thought he must have had to keep his arms up for many minutes while he was bandaged. There was a cut on his left cheek, a poorly aimed blow from Marcello, and the dull redness must have been the merbromin that Dr. Scognamiglio had used to disinfect it. They had once used it on my sister when she cut herself with a knife—her eyelids had quivered at the sight of the blood, only the whites of her eyes could be seen for a while, and then she fainted. The skin on Nicolas's cheek had darkened and lifted along the scar. The wounds gave him a grown-up look.

As I approached, he pretended not to see me and continued stroking the grass with his right hand.

"Are you Davide?" he asked, still gazing upward.

"Yes."

"Mastronardo said I had to help you paint the fence. But I don't know how to."

He tore a blade of grass and put it in his mouth. His words were direct, full of air, full of light. He spoke like the woman I had taken to Ciampate del Diavolo, like someone coming from a foreign language who's speaking Italian for the first time.

"I'll show you how it's done," I said.

"I don't care," he replied.

"Did Mastronardo tell you to do it, or not?"

"I'm Nicolas," he said.

I pretended not to know his name, never to have pronounced it correctly, not to know what letter it started with.

"If Mastronardo said you have to help, then you have to," I said.

"Okay, boss."

The same force that drew me to him pulled me back. In some way I was trying to delay getting to know him as long as I could.

I rummaged in the wheelbarrow. I had another paintbrush that needed to be soaked in order to soften the bristles.

"Bring a bucket of water," I said.

I found it a real struggle to order him about, but that was the only way of proving to myself that I could keep control.

He placed his hands on the ground and gave a push to lift himself up. Now that he was there in front of me, I saw once more the boy who had climbed down from the army truck. The two images now merged into one. I remembered him shading himself from the sun with a gesture that indicated both fragility and strength. Later I would try to imitate that pose with scarce results. His body and my first impression of him were exactly the same.

I was entering unknown territory. I felt a new urge to kiss Teresa and to spread myself over her. The picture of her bronzed skin made me feel dizzy. I felt an urge to rest my lips against hers, to feel their taste, but at the same time I'd have liked to resemble Nicolas. What I felt to be two different desires were, in truth, the same.

He went to the house and returned with a bucket. "Is this all right?"

I soaked the brush and tried to separate the bristles with my hands.

"I'll do it," Nicolas said.

"No," I replied.

I waited for the bristles to open, and when they were soft, I handed him the brush. I dipped mine into the paint and passed it over the slats of the fence in front of me.

"It's easy. There's nothing to it. You start here. I'll go there," I said, indicating the parts of the fencing that each of us needed to cover.

And as the number of shiny slats gradually increased, so did the distance between us. I felt happier not to be too close to him.

"Do you smoke?" he asked.

I shook my head.

He took out a cigarette and lit it.

He smoked and carried on painting.

"The ash is dropping into the paint," I said.

So Nicolas lay back on the grass again, as I had seen him when I first arrived. He blew the smoke up in the air. Nearly all the boys I knew pilfered their fathers' cigarettes or collected cigar ends and quietly smoked them. I thought Nicolas might have found cigarettes in the same way.

"I got it from Mastronardo when he came to call for me," he explained. "He leaves the packet on the table with his tools. It's easy to take them. He obviously doesn't bother to keep count. And anyway, these are horrible. Those you find in Naples are better."

This was the first thing I heard from his own lips about Naples: that their cigarettes were better than ours.

When he stood up again, a few blades of grass remained stuck to his back. He carried on painting the slats I had told him to do.

"Painting this fence reminds me of *The Adventures of Tom Sawyer*."

"Who's that?" I asked.

"Tom Sawyer? A character in a book. A boy who makes you think painting a fence is fun."

"Well, it's not," I answered.

We heard Mastronardo approach from a distance. Nicolas dug a small hole in the ground with his finger and buried the cigarette end.

"There were another two or three drags," he remarked.

Mastronardo appeared with one of his dogs, a brown short-haired mongrel that growled at everyone. Despite its tiny build, it played the perfect role of guard dog.

"How far have you got?" he asked.

He looked at my part, then at Nicolas's. He looked carefully at the wooden slats.

"This is all right," he said, looking at my part.

He put down the bag he had around his neck and went to Nicolas.

"That's no good, it's no good at all. I knew you weren't up to a job even as simple as this. I don't understand why they sent you. It's true, they're not dropping bombs here, and you know why? Because there's nothing to bomb."

"Come on, Mastronardo. I'll soon learn," Nicolas said.

"You should have already learned when I told you to milk the cows last week."

"But I did it."

"Yes, all right," Mastronardo retorted.

As he was talking to Nicolas, I saw a pack of cigarettes sticking out of the bag he had hung on a post toward my part of the fence. It was so close. I leaned across and pulled out the packet. The dog ran snarling toward me, but Mastronardo was so used to hearing it that he carried on talking to Nicolas. I dropped two cigarettes in among my tools.

"You have to finish your part like Davide's done his," Mastronardo said. Then he turned to me and took the bag. "You keep an eye on him."

"One is mine. I was the one who kept him away," Nicolas said, as soon as he had gone.

"Yes, but I was the one who took them."

"You're too slow. You must be more careful. He could have caught you."

I often wondered what would have happened if Don Aniello Panzer had caught me. Was it a serious crime? The things I stole were simple objects that cost hardly anything.

"Mastronardo holds nothing against us. He's a good man. He hasn't quite decided whether he likes us or not, like everyone in the village. And you, Davide, have you decided?"

"Whether I like you or not?"

"Yes."

I wasn't sure whether he was really interested in my answer. It was obviously a provocation.

"I have nothing against you. I just think that if you can't work the land, then there's no point you being here."

"That's what everyone says, and it's what we say too." He paused, then added: "Do you know why we're here?"

I remained silent.

"You're right not to answer," he said. "Not even we know why we're in this situation, and I'm not talking about being here. No one expected all of this."

He fingered a small scab on his chest.

"There's a list of things we can't do any longer."

"What list?"

"Listen to this," he said.

He put his hands on his hips, puffed up his chest, and imitated the voice of Mussolini, which everyone in the village had talked about but probably no one had actually heard. It was the same voice the podesta used when he climbed onto the platform to speak during the festival for the village patron saint.

"Patriots, from this moment on, marriage is forbidden between Italians and Jews. Do you want your daughter to marry a Jew? Your Duce has your interests at heart. It is forbidden for Jews to employ domestic servants of the Aryan race. You can't even imagine how many Jews have a maid. It is forbidden for Jewish children not converted to the Catholic faith to enroll in state schools, forbidden to attend university, forbidden to teach, forbidden to perform in the theater. Jews cannot work in banks, in insurance companies, cannot sell holy objects, cannot put death notices in newspapers. Do we really want to know when a Jew dies?"

His imitation made me laugh. If he'd been caught making fun of Mussolini, he'd have been sent to prison, and me with him.

Nicolas dropped his hands from his sides, and his voice returned to normal. "When we die, no one must know. In that way no one knows whether we die or run away. Because of your Duce, my father can no longer work, and I cannot go to school. Not to mention all those who have escaped abroad."

"To America?"

"You see, you know something too. Others hide away in the countryside, others say they're leaving, then shut themselves in their own homes. We weren't a separate community. We were those who went to buy bread each morning like everybody else.

Now we've become foreigners in the city in which we were born." He moved closer. "The Bristol Blenheim." He moved his open hand in the air as if it were an airplane and made the sound of an engine with his mouth. "I learned that name by heart after I saw a photograph in the newspaper. It's a small British airplane, fast, unbeatable. It's what they've used to bomb the areas around the port. But Naples has another city built underground, where people can hide. It's made of tufa, a yellow rock that looks like sponge. Such things don't happen here."

As he was talking, I noticed his long, spindly fingers, the opposite of mine, which are thick and stubby.

I didn't want him to die. I realized this. Now that I had stolen a cigarette for him, I really wanted him to stay alive.

"And school? You don't go any longer?"

"My father tells me about things. He does it because he fools himself that one day everything will go back to what it was before."

"Was he the one who told you the story of Tommaso Saverio?"

"Who?"

"The boy who paints the fence."

"Tom Sawyer?"

"Him."

"Yes, but those stories bore me. For the moment, I have to learn the things they tell us to do here: farm jobs, how to feed the animals."

"Do you reckon Mastronardo will send you off?"

He took the cigarette and lit it, shielding the flame of the wax match with his hand. After the first puff, there was a smell of mint.

"Is this your job?" he asked, without answering my question.

I looked at the fence before I understood what he meant.

"Is this what you do?" he repeated.

"I keep pigs."

"And how do you keep pigs?"

I didn't answer. He passed the cigarette to me.

"You have to hold the smoke in your belly for a second, then spit it out," he said.

I put the cigarette to my lips and inhaled for the first time in my life. But there would be no more. I would never learn to smoke. It burned my throat, then filled my mouth with the taste of wild mint. It wasn't a pleasant sensation. I handed it back to Nicolas, who took a puff to show me.

"I think the fencing is nearly finished," he said.

"Mastronardo won't come checking again," I said. "We can go."

"*Auf Wiedersehen*," he said, raising his hand, and went off holding the half cigarette that remained.

I never knew whether he looked upon me as a friend from the very start, but I felt he wasn't pushing me away. In Tora e Piccilli, he was just as alone as me.

At home, it was my mother who picked up the smell of the cigarette.

"Change your shirt, or your father will skin you alive," she said.

t was only many months later, when I had built up my store of words, that I could distinguish envy, curiosity, and pride among the dizzying range of emotions during those early days.

Nero was the only one who seemed to notice what was happening. He moved nervously inside his pen. He came from an age-old species and could read the signs sent out by the human body.

Did I have a new favorite? Was that what he felt?

"What are you complaining about—you're the only one with a pen to yourself," I told him.

I gave the animals as much water as I could and fed them. I waited for my mother and sister to go out, and when I was sure that no one would see me, I headed off for the workers' lodgings on Signora Ottavia's land. I walked along the path lined with oaks, past the trunk of a chestnut that had been split by lightning or by the January gales. I had to pass the colony of mushrooms that seemed like lookouts, at which point the oak trees formed a canopy overhead and followed you all the way.

When I arrived, I stayed hidden for a few minutes at the

clearing, and when I saw that no one was about, I went to the door and knocked.

"It's you," said Nicolas when he saw me.

I could see his father sitting in front of a book. The resemblance was more evident up close.

"Has Mastronardo said anything?" Nicolas asked, worried.

"No, nothing," I replied. "Can I come in?"

"What do you want?" he asked, moving aside to let me in. His father watched in silence from his chair. Inside, the kitchen was cold. I noticed the man was wearing a jacket. I went to the empty chair next to the one where I imagined Nicolas must have been sitting.

"Do you have some paper?" I asked.

The man pointed to a notebook. "Take that."

I opened it, found an empty page, and wrote my name. I wrote each letter as carefully as I could: the straight lines, the curves, and the dot over the *i* that Teresa had taught me. I showed it to the man, sliding the notebook over the table.

"I can write my name and other words," I said.

The man put on a small pair of spectacles with narrow oval frames the color of brass. His eyes seemed larger through the lenses.

"You write like a child though you're almost a man. Have you been to school?"

"No," I replied.

I heard the man breathe from his nose.

"Can you write *water*?" he asked.

"Yes."

"Show me."

He passed back the notebook. Nicolas came up behind me. I wrote what he had asked and showed it to him.

"That's not how you write it," he said. I had gotten it wrong but was happy all the same. His comment indicated that he had accepted me as a pupil. "You've written it in capital letters. Can you write normally?"

"No."

He reworded the question: "Do you know the difference between capital letters and normal handwriting?"

"No," I said again. "I know only a few words."

"And what words do you know?"

"I can write my name and the names of the pigs."

"What pigs are you talking about?"

"That's his job," Nicolas explained.

"And your pigs have names?" his father asked.

"Yes, like Nero."

"Why do you give them names?"

"If I call them, they turn around. And if they know they have a name, then they know they exist and they're a unique being, like you and your son, and like me."

The man took off his spectacles and held them for a moment.

"Mountains also have names," he said.

"They don't have ears to listen, so they don't know," I replied.

"Well, look what we have here. In the middle of all this mess we've found a young philosopher who doesn't know how to write *water* but talks about consciousness. I'm pleased to meet you. Do you live in the village?"

"We have a house on the other side of the woods."

"Davide is an important name for our people, did you know? He was a shepherd like you."

"I'm not a shepherd. I keep pigs. And then they call me all kinds of things because one leg is shorter than the other." I pointed to my leg to show him. "Hardly anyone calls me Davide. Sometimes they call me Furtunà, like my father. My last name is Buonasorte."

"Do you know the story of David and Goliath?"

"No, I'm sorry, I don't."

"You don't have to say sorry. It's the story of a shepherd who, through courage and intelligence, defeats a giant nine feet tall."

"Nine feet's a lot," I said.

"It's a story, which means it might not be true, and maybe the man was just normal height. But what's important is its meaning. Courage and smartness can enable you to perform incredible feats."

"Yes, but how does he kill him?"

"He knocks him out with a slingshot, shooting a pebble he had taken from a stream, then he finishes him off with his own sword."

"I can shoot stones. I can hit a wild boar in the woods while it's running away."

"Why do you go into the woods? Seen from here, they seem dangerous."

"Our house is on the other side. I have to go through the woods. I know them well. I never get lost."

"Why did you come here?"

"To ask you to show me how to write and how to read. I've heard this is a school."

"No, it's not a school. It's a house in the middle of the countryside full of mice. But if you want to, come. It's amazing—we've only just arrived, and these rumors are already about. We'll end up in front of a firing squad."

"I won't tell anyone," I said.

"Let's start with the letters. Write an *a* ten times on the first line, then a *b* on the second, and a *c* ten times on the third. Now Nicolas will show you how to write in cursive."

"I want to write in Italian, not in cursive."

Nicolas laughed, but it didn't matter if he was laughing at me. I was determined.

"I have to tell you something else."

"What's that, Davide?"

"I can't pay you. I have no money."

"Don't worry. We have no need of anything."

"Look," said Nicolas. He took the pen and showed me how to do what his father had told me to do. "Do you understand?"

I repeated each letter carefully. It was my first lesson, and I was anxious to do my best.

"Good," the man said. Then he turned to Nicolas: "And we can go back to what we were doing. You carry on through your lines."

And while I continued with my first real day at school, Nicolas went up to his father. He seemed hesitant.

"Carry on. You'll hardly be embarrassed by Davide?" his father asked.

Nicolas closed his eyes, seemed to be searching for something inside his head, then filled his lungs as if he were about to run or jump, and began: "Now is the winter of our discontent, made glorious summer by this sun of York; and all the clouds that lour'd upon our house, in the deep bosom of the ocean buried."

I too closed my eyes and tried to imagine the immensity and the unbearable weight of the deep bosom of the sea. To me it seemed those words were made flesh. I felt the weight of the enormous mass of water pressing against my chest, like when I'd had mumps and my mother had put her head on my chest to kiss me with her lips, which felt old and at the same time young. The deep bosom of the ocean was the deep place where those words were dragging me.

My hands shook. I was unable to carry on with my work.

"Once again, Nicolas. Let me hear how solemn and decisive those words are," his father said.

Nicolas then repeated what he had said, and each time his father added a new line. In this way, what he had to learn became longer and more complicated.

"Let me see," he said, looking at my work. "No, not like that. You must learn to control the letters on the page. Try to keep inside the lines. You mustn't go over the one above. That's why the lines are there."

I wrote a new *a*, this time smaller, trying to move the pen in the direction I wanted. Then another, and again.

"Like this?" I asked.

He took the sheet of paper and looked at it carefully to give importance to the work I had just done.

"That's fine, Davide. But now it's late. Please don't tell anyone you've been here."

"No, I'll tell no one," I replied.

"Do you have paper at home on which you can practice?"

"Don't worry, I have notebooks. When can I come again?"

"We're not allowed out of here," Nicolas said.

His tone had changed. It was no longer that of the deep bosom of the ocean, nor the one I had heard when he imitated Mussolini on Signora Ottavia's estate.

"He means you can come whenever you wish," his father explained.

I would have liked to have said sorry for what I'd done a

few evenings before. I had never experienced those feelings that came together at the same time and pulled in such opposing directions. Teresa told me this is why mountains are created, when two gigantic blocks of earth collide underground, and from that moment, something on the surface changes forever.

long the path back to the pigsty, I kept redrawing in the air the circular movement of the small *a* that stays between the lines. It's easy, I said, just keep your hand still. And now I had plunged in among the trees, swallowed up by the darkness, and began repeating "the deep bosom of the ocean." I tried to imitate Nicolas, but with my voice, the abyss was not to be seen, nor could I hear the weight of the sea pressing against my ribs. It was the first time I'd heard words as heavy as nine full buckets of water, and that made my knees bend.

I reached the pigsty.

My father was sitting outside. When he heard my footsteps, he turned in my direction. I had never seen him look so furious. His face was like the rock at the beginning of our vegetable patch: old, impenetrable.

He took me by the shirt and dragged me into the sty.

"They saw you going to the Jews."

He flung me to the ground, pushing against my chest in the very same place where I had felt the ocean.

"Look, look," he said.

I saw the empty pen.

Nero had escaped. He had broken one of the slats and reached the entrance. My father dragged me into pen number five. I defended myself as well as I could. Furtunà was used to dealing with animals twice his weight. He would frighten them by shouting and fixing them in the eye. Fear is a language that everyone understands.

He pushed me, and the weight of his body knocked me down. We had the same strength, we could have fought, but I didn't move a finger. I was obeying an ancient commandment according to which fathers are permitted, but sons are not. So long as we were both on this earth, the fact that he and I were father and son would remain unchanged.

I stood and planted my good leg into the ground like a pillar. That was all I did—resist without raising a hand. But my effort was to no avail. He lifted me and threw me into the fence.

"Now I'll go looking for him, and I swear I'll find him. You sleep here tonight. If you dare to move, you'll see what'll happen."

I remained alone with the pigs. The straw was still warm, a sign that Nero hadn't escaped for long. In a certain sense his body was still there in the pigsty. I closed my eyes: The deep bosom of the ocean still dominated my mind.

I stretched out. Nero's warmth enveloped me. The coldness had solidified his excrement, and I pushed it away with my hands. The pigs went silent. I fell asleep.

During the night I was woken by my mother. She was crying. I'm not sure whether out of shame that I was sleeping with the pigs or because my father and I had been fighting.

I pretended to sleep. I had nothing to tell her, nor did I want to listen. I felt neither pain nor anger. I had no feeling toward her. She had spent her whole life obeying first her mother and then my father, never exerting any will of her own, and this for me was an unpardonable sin. If we cannot alter our own destiny, we are nothing.

She moved toward the door without making a sound, and I saw her pale thin figure disappear into the darkness.

The next morning at dawn, I heard squealing. An excruciating sound, a body swollen with fear, begging for mercy. I emerged from the pen with my legs quivering, praying that I was mistaken. I had already heard too many pigs die.

I found Nero strung up by his hind legs, his throat slit.

The blood had drained into a puddle. His mouth was open, his eyes all white. The rope still vibrated in remembrance of his frenzy. A mangy cat had come out from the woods to watch. I kept vigil over the corpse throughout the day.

Night returned. My father was nowhere to be seen. I lost my senses. The pain was too great to bear. When I reopened my eyes, I found myself in bed in my room with a cloth over my forehead stuffed with slices of potato, for my fever had increased. I had slept two consecutive days, hearing the words "in the deep bosom of the ocean" hundreds of times over, superimposed on the image of Nero strung up with his throat cut.

When I was strong enough to get up, there was no trace of Nero. His carcass must have been sold at the market.

ON THE NIGHT MY FATHER KILLED NERO, I DECIDED WE would no longer be father and son. I decided to sever all ties with my family. I did not belong to them, nor did they belong to me. Only in that way would the death of the greatest pig Tora e Piccilli had ever seen not have been in vain.

I remained closed in the house for the whole week. I felt weak and my legs trembled, as if that death had been transferred into my own bed and I were sleeping beside it every night. My body tried to keep hold of Nero's strength and drive out death. I could still feel a part of life pulsating somewhere.

My mother kept bringing bread and milk to my bed, and not once in seven days did my father ask after me. He must have understood that such an action, for me, was the point of no return. The priest once preached from the altar that God had created the world in seven days; it had taken me the same time to destroy it. That pain had liberated me. The death of Nero marked the end of fear and submission. His courage had passed to me through the sight of his blood and the contemplation of his hanging carcass. I had kept vigil, and now his spirit possessed me. On that day I was born a second time.

During that week, I wrote out the letters that Nicolas's father had shown me, and when my brain could no longer control my lips, I said aloud: "Now is the winter of our discontent, made glorious summer by this sun of York; and all the clouds that lour'd upon our house, in the deep bosom of the ocean buried."

I had never gone further than Tora-Presenzano station, yet I was talking about the sun of York, and as I repeated those words, I saw the clouds gather and felt myself sink under the immense mass of water that pushed me into somewhere as inaccessible as a mother's womb.

The meaning wasn't clear to me, but I understood the deep bosom of the ocean was death that enveloped and swallowed you in a deep well, from which no one had ever escaped. That must have been what Nero felt just a few moments before my father plunged in the blade. He too must have felt the world opening while his life slipped away.

I returned to the pigsty on the eighth day. Nero's spirit had left me, his soul had abandoned the earth, and now both he and I were different, both filled with grief, and both stronger.

'VE BEEN waiting for you," Nicolas said.

"I've been ill."

"What was wrong?"

"I had a fever."

He put his hands on my forehead.

"It's been over a week," he said.

"That's how long it takes to go."

"Did you take any medicine?"

"It goes by itself."

"Maybe that's true for horses. My father was asking about you."

"What did you tell him?"

"That I didn't know where to find you."

"I've done the homework. I want to try more difficult things now."

"More difficult than what?"

"Than the letters I had to write."

I had come across him on the path by the stream, not far from where he lived. From the time he arrived with his father, he had been exploring the surrounding area. I thought he would gradually move further each day to extend the territory he knew, but I was wrong. That was what I would have done, but Nicolas didn't think like that.

"I can come now—my father's not around."

"Let's go," he said.

His father was cooking when we arrived, and there was a smell of stewed vegetables.

"Look who's here, our young philosopher. I thought perhaps you weren't coming back. I'd have been sorry if you hadn't. I can recognize a good pupil straightaway. I wanted to ask Mastronardo, but we thought it best not to."

"It's better if you don't come to my house," I said.

"At the moment it's better for us not to be seen at anyone's house, but we're sure things will improve after a few days. You are good people. And we are too, aren't we, Nicolas?"

Nicolas made no reply. That question must have been part of a conversation they had started between themselves.

"I've had a fever," I said.

"That's the excuse my pupils always gave. You're all the same—in the city, in the countryside. Have you recovered?"

"It wasn't a lie. It's gone now."

"Have you done your homework?"

"I've done it all."

He was keeping an eye on the pot on the fire. "Come, Nicolas, you can look after this."

Nicolas began stirring the contents with a large wooden spoon. He didn't seem too pleased to do it.

"Let me see," said the father.

I handed him the paper, and he looked carefully at the

sequence of letters. "They look like clothes hanging on the line to dry. Look how they all slope to one side. I might get seasick. But you've done very well."

"I never know when you're serious and when you're making fun of me," I said.

"I'm always serious, but lighthearted with it, and this confuses people."

"I want to write *water*, *stone*, *earth*, *pigs*, *river*, and *bread*."

He wrote down these words and handed me the pen. I copied them carefully, then read them aloud, one after the other.

"Good," he remarked.

"There's another thing," I said, taking a breath. "*The deep bosom*."

"I don't understand," he said, with a look of puzzlement.

"What Nicolas said last time."

Nicolas began to recite with his back to us, still stirring the soup: "Now is the winter of our discontent, made glorious summer by this sun of York; and all the clouds that lour'd upon our house, in the deep bosom of the ocean buried."

"Yes, that," I said.

"Why?" asked Nicolas. "What about it?"

"They're new words. They say things I never thought could be heard. I know that the deep bosom of the sea doesn't exist, but I seem to feel the weight of the water."

"Do you want to repeat it with me?" Nicolas asked.

My legs were shaking.

"All right," I said.

"Now is the winter of our discontent," he began.

"Now is the winter of our discontent," I repeated.

"Made glorious summer by this sun of York."

"Made glorious summer by this sun of York."

"And all the clouds that lour'd upon our house."

"And all the clouds that lour'd upon our house."

"Finish the sentence by yourself," said Nicolas.

I closed my eyes and tried to remember how he had said it a moment before with his back to us. "In the deep bosom of the ocean buried."

While I was intoxicated by that first success, I thought of Nero, who was now dead because of those new words I had heard.

That evening I returned home knowing how to write *bread*, *earth*, *nails*, *eat*, and other things.

A few days later, *ocean*, *death*, *father*, *Nero*, and *deep* appeared in the notebook.

Other Jews came later to Tora e Piccilli. They came voluntarily, having heard stories from others who had been sent there.

Life in the village was tedious. There was nothing but land and animals, trees and rocks, and the only instance of violence to have occurred had been classified as an isolated incident, carried out perhaps by a few irresponsible children.

It's not true that we heard nothing about the bombings. News reached us here too. But what we didn't know about was the fear they brought and the anxious rush to the air-raid shelters and the uncertainty about what you would find when the sirens went quiet. So others had come spontaneously.

"Why should they bomb our sheep?" the old men would ask. "Could a bomb ever cost less than a sheep? If they really want to frighten us, they should throw wolves."

The first feelings of suspicion against the Jews were soon overcome. The Fascist propaganda had described them for what they were not, and the enemies of the regime turned out to be harmless individuals who spoke good Italian and had delicate hands through never having done a day's work on the land. The people of Tora e Piccilli soon accepted them as if they had always been part of the community, and when they weren't doing the tasks given to them, they wandered about feeling quite safe.

For me, of course, it was different.

I carried on visiting Nicolas's house without my father knowing. I knew what hours he kept and knew when I could leave the pigsty without being seen. If there was one person at Tora e Piccilli who lived a truly secret life, it was me.

After Nero's death I was no longer frightened of punishment. There was nothing else my father could take away from me. The fury of his action had been a bad move for him. Now I was free. I had already paid the highest price. I still lived at my father's house, for I had nowhere else to go, but I began thinking about an independent life. Somewhere small with a few animals to look after. It was the sweetest thought, and it comforted me in the few moments before I fell asleep. A vegetable patch of my own was another thought that consoled me. No more animals to think of as meat or merchandise. In my father's house, this was a most revolutionary idea.

I cherished what I called "solitude" only for lack of the exact word, which Nicolas suggested a few days later. The word was *independence*. To escape from Tora e Piccilli, disappearing without a trace. I didn't yet know how it would happen but knew only that it would.

The other people who attended the secret school stopped coming after a few days and, apart from Nicolas, I remained the only pupil. This cheered me up, and I thought the air of intimacy might help me find some way ahead.

I spent more and more time with Nicolas. I learned his gestures and his words. I moved my arms like him. We hunted lizards, which we then set free. I taught him which families the fields belonged to and drew a map for him. It was better for us not to be seen together in the village, so he went off by himself for long walks. I mistakenly imagined he would follow my directions, but he had no fear of losing himself and walking for hours, gathering stems of grass to chew. I admired those walks with no destination and his sudden changes of direction, not because his legs were more agile than mine, but because I had seen how he greeted people when he met them. His was a beauty difficult to explain, certainly for someone like me who had so few words to describe it. I could only remain with him and flatter myself that something would pass to me, never imagining, not even once, that Nicolas himself might be taking something of mine.

ON SUNDAY MORNINGS WE WENT TO CHURCH. CHURCH and fascism were compulsory for all villages like ours. We had to depend on something, or someone—fearful, therefore governable. The two oldest institutions in my life were both founded on fear.

We crossed through the outer part of the woods and turned onto the lane, which was a track worn by our own footsteps. Rosetta at that point would start humming a tune. As we left the track, we could hear our feet on the stones. Of all of us, mine sounded different.

In the village they called me many names: *scartiello*, humpback; *scanna puorco*, swine slayer; *sciancatu*, hop-along; *abbuccato*, crook-shank; or *guallaruso*, bandy-legs.

"Walk properly," my father would say.

The sound of my right foot grew louder as it dragged on the cobbles until it became unbearable even for me.

"I can't do any better than this."

He died of shame. After Nero's death, I no longer felt it.

"Lift your feet," he hissed.

I had watched him kill piglets born with any kind of deformity. He resolved the problem with a knife, and no hesitation. Some mothers wouldn't notice, while others would go mad and cry for a whole night.

It was only when we saw the bell tower and other folks that he gave up telling me to walk properly.

Our Sunday clothes were what our parents had passed down to us. We could have bought new ones, even at the Tuesday cloth market at Grottola. I hated putting my legs into what had been the trousers of my father's wedding suit. Every Sunday I turned into the man in the photograph my mother kept by her bed.

While the priest was talking, however hard I tried, my own thoughts intervened, and when the people lined up to take the host, I went too, even though I hadn't been to confession. Don Mariano said it was a terrible sin. But for Teresa and me it was a kind of game.

Every family had a pew in church with their own name. We had one too. It was a luxury we could afford because my grandmother had bought the name plaque before she died. She'd had the names of her own family and my grandfather's family inscribed so as to leave that single inheritance to both branches.

I went to the pew in front of ours, which was not yet occupied.

"What are you doing?" my father muttered, having just made a sign of the cross.

I put my finger on the name plaque and began to read as it ran over each letter: "In memory of the Panzilmo family."

The Panzilmo family lived next to the church. There was a green gate that I peered through each time I passed, into the clean and tidy courtyard with a small chicken pen at the far end, its wooden slats neatly painted. While my father motioned me back to our pew, I moved on to the next one: "By kind donation of the Rocchito-Tusso family."

Do you read the hyphen? I'd have to ask Nicolas.

They owned the grocery store and sold pasta in a conical paper bag they called a *cuoppo*.

I knew both families well, and now that I knew how they wrote their names, I felt I knew something more.

I returned to our pew.

My father took me by the arm and squeezed it. My mother put her hand to her mouth. She always did this when she was afraid. I didn't resist. He seemed to have no further strength. I waited immobile until his grip weakened.

The bell sounded. The priest stepped forward. There was an altar boy two paces in front of him who swung the censer like a pendulum. When the chain reached the furthest extent of its movement, a small cloud of smoke appeared through the holes in the upper part. As a child, I thought it was the aroma of God.

The priest moved up the nave.

I recited a prayer in our dialect for Nero's soul. This language so like that of the land, these words so like the noises of the animals, seemed the only way of conversing with the souls of dead beasts.

Teresa and her family were on the other side. When she saw me, she got up from her pew and crossed the aisle, making no sign of the cross. I did the same, ignoring my father's reaction.

"I could take no more of it," she said when I joined her outside.

I hadn't seen her for a while and hadn't told her what had

happened to Nero, nor that I'd decided I was no longer part of my family. Nor did she know anything about Nicolas or his father or the secret school I went to at the end of the path through the oaks.

"Why don't you come to see me anymore?" she asked.

I didn't answer.

"You seem different," she continued. "I can't say how."

I could also feel this change.

"I'm wearing the same clothes," I replied.

She looked at my familiar trousers. "I can see. That wasn't what I meant."

I moved closer to her, the only person in the village I trusted. She was my own little church.

"I've seen him," she said.

"Who?" I asked. I already knew the answer.

"The boy they're talking about in the village."

How could I have failed to imagine that other people hadn't been overwhelmed by him too?

"Do you want to come? You can talk to him if you want," I said.

"You know him?"

"Do you want to go and see Nicolas?" I repeated, pronouncing his name as I had heard his father say it.

"Why, you know him?"

"Just tell me if you want to go."

Teresa took a step back. She had to choose between returning to the church and Nicolas. It took two seconds, the length of a whole life.

"Now?" she asked, seeing her mother in the distance preparing to leave after the last blessing.

"Now."

"All right," Teresa said.

"Let's go."

We didn't know that we were like the moths that fly too close to the flame, attracted by the splendor of the light, and end up with their wings burned in that kind of last dance in which joy overcomes fear.

WE WALKED IN SILENCE. TERESA SOMETIMES OVERTOOK me, giving me the chance to study her from behind. I recognized the perfection of her figure, silhouetted against the sun. I had seen the outline of her figure transform itself over the years: Her shapes that had once been sharp and regular were now inhabited by curves. I had always thought that she walked faster than me because there was an innate kind of competition in her. It must have been the same at school, and this divided her class in two: those who wanted her as a friend, and those who saw her as an enemy. Her attitude required a choice.

At several points along the path, she had to lift her dress to get past bushes that might have torn it. It wasn't the first time I had seen her legs. My feelings for her had changed, like everything around me.

"Do you want me to go slower?" she asked.

"I'll manage."

"Sorry, I shouldn't have asked."

"It doesn't matter."

When we reached the workers' lodgings on Signora Ottavia's land, Nicolas was bent over, pulling weeds from the ground. We could see his shoulder muscles tight beneath his skin. Any trace of aggression seemed to have gone.

A FEW YEARS BEFORE, I HAD A TIN BALLERINA THAT REvolved on a platform. When it was wound up, it turned smoothly at first, then in nervous judders, and stopped halfway. You had to move it by hand, back to the point where it had started. She wore out. She too must have had one shorter leg.

One night I took it apart to look at the mechanism that made her dance, and as soon as I lifted it up, the springs and gears shot out. I tried repairing it, and that same night I dug a hole and buried it behind the pigsty. Certain mechanisms are mysterious and, once opened, are ruined. Everything becomes fragile in the light.

"CIAO, DAVIDE," NICOLAS SAID WHEN HE SAW US.

I felt proud that he had used my name in front of Teresa and that he was the first to speak. We approached.

Nicolas was still looking down, pretending that I was alone.

"This is Teresa," I said.

He stood up, wiped his hands on his worn trousers, and offered his right hand to Teresa.

"Fräulein," he said, miming a bow.

"Ciao," Teresa replied.

They shook hands.

"Where are you going?" Nicolas asked.

"We were taking a walk," I said.

He was our destination. There was nowhere in the area to go to, apart from farms where the farmers or their dogs would have chased us away.

"No pigs today?"

"Later," I replied.

"I'll come along."

"Can you?"

He looked toward Signora Ottavia's house. "No one will notice."

"Let's go, then," Teresa said, starting to run.

Nicolas and I looked at each other and followed. Teresa slowed down, but I hobbled along all the same. It was the first time I had seen Nicolas running. He could have caught up with her in a few strides, to do what she had always done, which was trying to win to show who was the best at everything. Instead, he let her stay at the head of the small expedition, following behind. I tripped over a root, fell, grazed my hands, and neither Nicolas nor Teresa noticed. I got up with my skin bruised and managed to catch them up.

The late October day was hot. The midmorning sun shone right above our heads. We cut through Signora Ottavia's fields and carried on through the woods. Our running startled the birds. We didn't yet know where we were going, nor what we were escaping from. We were sure only of our young bodies.

I caught up with them. They had stopped, both gripping their legs to catch their breath back. The coolness of the water reached our faces.

"What's this called?" Nicolas asked, still bent over his knees.

"It's the river," Teresa said.

"It's no more than a stream. You say that because you've never seen a river, right?"

"I've seen the sea," Teresa replied.

"You can see it from my house for that matter. In fact, every house in Naples can see the sea. And do you know something else? You can't bomb the sea. One day they will rebuild everything, but not the sea. War, for the sea, is just a joke."

"Come," Teresa said, after a few moments' silence.

We continued along the bank. The ground sank at various points, and we could see the silvery bodies of fish flitting and darting away to hide in murkier waters.

"Here we are."

We arrived at the wooden platform used by fishermen. I knew because my father was one of those who had built it, and from his description it had seemed like a great feat of engineering when, in fact, on closer inspection, it was a few planks nailed together that had unaccountably survived the passage of time. I used to go there occasionally. I had sometimes seen an old man with a rod staring at a float that never moved, or children with nets, hoping to catch a few fish.

"Do you fish here?" Nicolas asked.

"No," said Teresa. "My grandpa would sometimes come. It was hours before anything took the bait. The fish are small around here. They eat so many insects that they're not bothered about the worms on the hook."

"We could try it some time," Nicolas said.

"Not today," Teresa said.

"And what shall we do?"

We all looked at the expanse of water flowing beneath our feet. It wasn't far below but looking down made me dizzy. With our heads leaning over the edge of the platform, our bodies were drawn off balance, and the water and the void exerted a mysterious attraction.

"Let's dive in," said Teresa.

"What?" Nicolas asked.

Teresa took a step back, almost to the center of the platform, then let her pink Sunday dress slip down and stood in her underpants and bra. She moved toward the edge.

"Don't do it," I said.

I felt so scared that I couldn't keep quiet. I distinctly remember my pathetic voice, which tried to control what I would one day discover to be the most noble of human feelings: courage.

Teresa was half-naked before the two of us. The white flesh of her back. Her round, plump breasts covered by a thin layer of cloth. She looked again toward the water, then took two steps back without turning, closed her eyes to focus on what she was about to do, and took a short run. When her feet left the platform, I saw them flail in the air for a few moments, then heard the splash as she reached the water. We looked down at the point where she had dived. Teresa had been swallowed by the water beneath our eyes. A layer of white bubbles appeared on the surface.

Teresa had once told me, in describing the color of wisteria, *glicine*, which was also her surname, that I had to imagine violets kept in water for two days. Water was an element that belonged to her and to which she would return. She waited a few seconds too long to resurface, so that fear began to emerge in our faces. Her hair clung to her face, and she wiped the water away with her hands. She covered her breasts. Her pink nipples were now visible where whiteness had been.

"Come!" she shouted. "It's your turn!"

She was smiling and shouting like someone who had nothing more in life to fear.

Nicolas took his trousers off and stood in his underpants.

"Here I am," he shouted.

Like Teresa, he took a short run and jumped from the platform. This time the jump was accompanied by a yell. An indeterminate sound, halfway between an *a* and an *e*, and I could see the two letters written in my notebook. He entered the water clumsily. The position of his arms and legs stopped him from sinking. He took two strokes toward Teresa.

"Come, Davide, it's your turn," he said.

I took off my shirt and trousers. I was now in my underpants like them, and turned to face away from the platform, paralyzed with fear. With my legs I could move neither forward nor back.

"Come, Davide." This time it was Teresa who spoke.

For as long as I had known her, I had never seen her smile as much as she was smiling now in the water with Nicolas.

"Just jump," they said, this time together, as if they were trying to synchronize their voices.

If I hadn't jumped, my ghost would have remained on that wooden platform forever at the far end of the woods. I took a run and felt the intoxication of the void.

My life began with that jump.

t was Teresa who taught me the word *cianfrusaglie*, junk. It's a word full of curves, of hidden indentations, ups and downs—like the village that went up from the archway to the tower. She had read it in a book that an aunt from Potenza had given her for her first communion, and like all the words she underlined or wrote in her notebook of special words, she had used it one afternoon at the ropeworks as naturally as someone who has a vocabulary with the right word for everything. To get to school she took the bus, but by using words like that it seemed she had known the whole world. When I tried to pronounce it, I heard bits of metal clanging together.

"That's right. You have to hear the metal," she said.

The only place at Tora e Piccilli where you could see *cianfrusaglie* was Don Aniello Panzer's truck. He kept it in a green box next to the saucepans sold as wedding gifts for young girls about to marry. Village daughters would never have considered peering into that box full of dirty, broken, secondhand objects he had probably collected from the garbage bins of Naples and carried around the villages, passing them off as rarities. They were objects that had already had a wretched life and were now to be found in Don Aniello Panzer's box, like the pigs we took to market knowing that after that journey, for them, there was no further hope.

Small round pairs of curved spectacles with no lenses, keys with a lion's head that opened doors of unknown houses, scales with brass weights. It was here among that rust-diseased metal that I saw the ballerina. She was covered by grubbier objects. *Cianfrusaglie* now meant the sea that submerges, the snow that covers, the fog that obscures. I slipped her into my bag, and by stealing her, I saved her.

Don Aniello Panzer's vanity was his weakness. The prouder he was of his goods, of the power of his truck as it climbed to the highest villages, and of all he had witnessed in his life, the more distracted he became. I reckon people stole things from him at every market.

At home I used some pincers instead of the metal key that had probably been left in the previous owner's pocket. I shook it inside until I found the point to wind it up. When I set it going, the ballerina moved. I watched her movements and learned the exact point at which she made a clumsy jolt that made her seem like a beginner. This was what I liked about her: She had a value, even if she had ended up in the junk box. She was suspended on a small metal rod, yet I wondered whether the irregular movements were due to her legs not being the same size. I stared at her during the night and imagined how she must have been when she was new, perfect as she spun around and in her final bow, while a tune must have come out of the tin stage that now sounded like bits of glass.

I dreamed about her the night after I had buried her. She asked to be wrapped in a cloth because she didn't want the soil on her face. She called me by my name.

The next day I found a piece of cloth and went digging in the place that I remembered. I cleaned her face, wiping away soil and tears, then wrapped her as I did with the corpses of dead birds that I sometimes found frozen in the fields.

e stayed there on the grass to dry our hair. In the silence I listened to the running water as the tobacco of Nicolas's cigarette burned in the air. He filled his lungs with smoke and slowly let it out, holding it in his chest as long as possible. He was sitting with his knees bent, looking into the distance. October was mild. Fall still seemed far away.

I was stretched out, gazing at Teresa, who had gone to lay down a few yards further on. Now and then she took a length of hair and squeezed it, with her face toward the sun. I was looking at parts of her body that I had only imagined.

She kept closing her eyes, as if she still wanted to protect them from the water. In that kind of abandonment, she seemed younger than her sixteen years.

The memory of her taking off her dress gave me an erection. I turned onto my stomach.

I was confusing my youth with the Sunday heat that was slowly warming us. It was a promise of something that would come to be.

After a while, Teresa dressed again, squatting as she did so. I turned away.

Nicolas remained with his chest uncovered. His shirt was on the grass. We had both jumped in, but our reasons were so different that it seemed we hadn't bathed in the same water.

We remained silent for a space of time that seemed as long as the end of a summer.

"How long will you be staying here?" Teresa asked Nicolas.

"I don't know. No one knows exactly. We don't even know the real reason why we're here."

"Don't you like it?" she asked.

"We had a life in Naples. I went to school. I had the theater. My father taught. We've had no news of my mother and my sisters for days."

"What are your sisters called?"

"Miriam and Rachele."

"Are they older or younger than you?"

"Both, in the sense that they're younger but behave as if they're older."

"Do they adore you?"

Teresa's question embarrassed me.

"No," Nicolas said, "I don't think so."

"I think they do, or maybe they're jealous," Teresa said.

"There's no such thing as jealousy between brothers and sisters," Nicolas said.

"All the same, you know what I mean."

A mother, two sisters. Nicolas's world was starting to become more complex, more extensive. For the time I had known him, my only wish was for him to teach me how to be like him, with no particular interest in his life. That disarming beauty, courtesy, refinement, artistic ambition, and, last of all, the racial persecution that drove him toward martyrdom. Nicolas lived exactly in the way I imagined him. It was no contradiction, just very hard to explain. But now I saw how naturally Teresa was interested in his life in Naples, and the bourgeois, coquettish attention she gave as she listened to him. His sisters became the object of her questions, as if she had chosen not to look straight at the sunlight but to reconstruct it by starting from the shadows.

"Are you afraid?" Teresa asked Nicolas, without specifying of what.

Nicolas looked for another cigarette, lit it, inhaled, then said, "I'm afraid like everyone. I don't like it. I don't like being ruled."

"Fear takes hold of you. You can't control it," Teresa said.

"This is true for animals and certain kinds of people. I try not to be like either of them."

Nicolas stood up. He seemed disturbed by what Teresa had said. I had a sudden feeling of growing at a vertiginous pace. In their mouths, simple familiar words were being replaced by other strange words that had infinitely more complex meanings.

"Here in Tora, nothing ever happens, and nothing will ever happen, even to you and your father," Teresa said. "They're good people, farmers mostly. Work is all they know. They make no distinction between one person and another."

"There were many good people where we lived too. Then they suddenly turned their backs on us. It happened gradually, without our noticing."

Nicolas waited for a response, but Teresa continued to listen in a silence filled with admiration.

"Now no one knows what will happen next," Nicolas continued. "The people here have accepted us, and we're comfortable on the farm." After a pause, he added: "I was attacked during the early days."

"Who by?" Teresa asked.

"They were people just as frightened as me. Not even they understand all this."

There was something revolutionary about him, in the simplicity with which he gave us access to his fear and to his life.

"Earlier you talked about the theater," Teresa said.

"In Naples I joined a theater company."

"Is that what you want to be, an actor?"

"I don't know yet. I don't know what's going on in the world, let alone what I want to be."

"In Tora e Piccilli no one cares about such things," Teresa said, gesticulating passionately, angrily. "People here just talk about sheep, pigs, rabbits. When a calf that is bigger than normal is born, the news goes around the whole village. A chicken with three wings was once hatched, and everyone thought it meant the end of the world. Half of the village went to the priest; the other half to the local witch."

Nicolas laughed.

"It's the countryside. That's how it is. These are real people who don't need theater," Nicolas said. "There's something good about it too."

"We live in the Middle Ages," Teresa said.

I was with them, lying in the sun, but unable to join the conversation. Never, since I was born, had I heard two people talking without one of them trying to get the better of the other or trying to prove they were right.

"My father says I have to keep practicing the monologue from *Richard III.*" Nicolas sighed. "He says words are a way of taking your mind off what's going on, but . . ."

"Carry on," Teresa said.

"But I don't agree. I don't want to replace truth with theater. Without truth, theater can't exist."

We remained silent, absorbing those last words.

"Let's go," Teresa said at last.

"My hair is still wet," I protested. I could have stayed there forever.

"Come on, Davide. It's Sunday, a holiday."

"Where shall we go?" Nicolas asked.

"To the station. It's quite a walk."

"I saw it. We went past when they brought us here."

"It won't take long if we cut through the fields."

So we began walking.

The couples alternated along the way. Me and Teresa, Teresa and Nicolas, me and Nicolas.

When we arrived, Teresa looked at the timetable.

"If we want to see a train, we'll have to wait two hours."

We sat on a low wall staring at the rails. Nicolas and I had gone there only because she'd asked us, and she was the only one disappointed.

A man emerged from the station and yelled that we had to go. So we got up and walked in the sun along a wall, each close to the other. Our hair still had the aroma of stream water.

went back to see Nicolas two days after our bath in the stream. My father had gone to Caserta, and I could move about as I wished. The more time he spent at Fascist meetings, the more study time I had at Nicolas's house. My progress was directly proportional to his devotion to Mussolini. The Duce took care of me in that way. I began to think my father had ambitions within the Fascist Party and wanted to apply his organization of the pigsty to the whole village of Tora e Piccilli.

I crossed the woods to reach Signora Ottavia's estate. I now knew every detail of their house, the sound of the window as it closed, the wooden spoon as it scraped the pot of boiling soup that was their only meal.

Nicolas's father opened the door.

"Good morning, *signore*."

"Don't call me *signore*. Call me Gioacchino. There's bread on the table. Mastronardo brought it for us. He said it was left over." He disappeared along the corridor looking for something while I stayed in the kitchen with the bread and the books on the table.

"I've written all the words," I said when he returned.

"Well done. Let me see."

I handed him the notebook.

"Isn't Nicolas here?" I asked as he read.

"He had a fever yesterday. He's still in bed, but he's improving now. I think the summer lasts longer here in the countryside, and he spends the whole day in a cotton undershirt. He's in his room. Go and say hello. He'll be pleased."

It was a brick-built house that must once have been servants' quarters. The small corridor leading to the bedroom was dark, and a patch of mold could be seen along the wall.

I had never been to Nicolas's room and wondered why I had never had the curiosity until then. I knocked on the door and opened it without waiting for a reply. He was asleep, wrapped in a blanket, visibly weak. His lips were lighter than usual and his face pallid. In the room there was just a bed. It seemed suspended along the wall, a raft floating at the water's edge. My way of seeing was changing. I was aware of things I wouldn't have noticed until a few weeks before. Bed, clothing, untidy kitchen. Everything was becoming new and interesting. Every object was struck by a new light.

The window had no curtains. There were books on the floor, and his clothes, which I had learned to recognize, were on a chair in the corner.

I left before he woke. I didn't want him to catch me in his room.

"Did you see him?" Gioacchino asked.

"He's asleep."

I wondered if the fever had been caused from diving into the chilly stream water or from seeing Teresa in her underpants.

"In the meantime, I've looked at what you have written. You've done well. There are many new words too."

"I found them written on a piece of paper."

"Do you have it with you?"

"Yes."

"Let me see."

The paper had been folded several times. I kept it in my front trouser pocket.

Gioacchino unfolded it and read it.

"It's Fascist propaganda," he said.

"I know what it is."

"I don't want this stuff in our house."

"Sorry, I used it to copy down what was written there. I don't think like they do, otherwise I wouldn't be here."

We had no books or magazines at home. My father brought those leaflets back with him. I had seen what went on during the meetings. There was always someone who handed them out. Somewhere in them was a picture of Mussolini doing everyday tasks.

"All right," Gioacchino said, "now let's carry on with our work. Words are always the same. What's important is how they are used. Let's read what is written on it."

So the first text I studied was a leaflet setting out the principles of the racial laws, and it was a Jewish teacher who explained what they meant. Nicolas had told me about them at the very start of our friendship, but now that I saw the words in writing, I could understand how those lies were even beginning to take root. As I read them, I realized there was no such thing as a good or a bad word. *Trap*, *heart*, *hole*, *bus*, *breast*, *back*, *mouth*. Everything was dependent on actions.

NICOLAS'S RECOVERY TOOK A WEEK. I LEARNED THAT A beautiful body could also be fragile, and that beauty and fragility were indeed intimately connected. It was during the third afternoon of Nicolas's illness that Teresa came looking for me in the pigsty.

"How is he?" she asked.

"His father said he's getting better."

"It was my fault," she said. "I shouldn't have insisted on that stupid bathing. I don't know how the idea ever came into my head. I should have realized Nicolas wasn't used to our way of life."

"You and I have never gone bathing together," I said.

"He's used to the city."

That was the way she took the blame. It was another of her shows of strength, like whipping the pharmacist's son or undressing in front of Nicolas and me. She was ready to take the blame for the whole of humanity.

"Gioacchino said Nicolas would spend another ten days at home," I lied. "He doesn't want to risk him getting ill again."

That night I saw her once more in my dream, undressing over and again. She was trapped in one single possible movement, like the ballerina on the tin box. I felt the heat of the sun, saw the lizards warming themselves, and saw her emerging from the circle of clothes that were heaped at her feet. And as I stretched my hand out to touch her, I opened my eyes, for I was frightened that my desire might somehow be fulfilled.

Without Nicolas, I spent those days carrying a kind of pain behind me. I wasn't sure what it was that hurt me: my leg, the short one or the good one, my arm, my head, or my lungs, like those of my father. It was a feeling unlike anything I had ever felt before, and it made me weak.

The next day I returned with my father to the market. It was our first outing together since the death of Nero. If I had wanted to list everything that had changed since Nicolas's arrival at Tora, I wouldn't have known where to start. I looked for confirmation in the change I saw in the trees along the way, but I didn't find it because it was the roots that were changing.

I arrived at the market with the handcart, pushing one of the pigs on it that had to be delivered to its new owner.

We waited at the usual place, and meanwhile I looked at the people around. There was nearly the whole village, and those few I didn't recognize certainly came from nearby.

"Is this the one?" the man we'd come to meet asked my father. He felt the pig along its back to check it was well, then examined its ears and trotters. Furtunà had a good reputation as a breeder and would never have cheated anyone. He was known in the village for his hard work and for those principles that ought to have been shared by all Italians. After that brief investigation, the man handed over the money.

"Goodbye, *mastu* Biagio," my father said. He put the money into his front pocket, then turned to me.

"We need to make the pigsty bigger. I want more animals."

"And what will you do with them?"

"We'll expand. Have you seen what Veneruso has done?"

"And where will you put them?"

"We'll build another sty. We'll knock down the old one and make space. The pens must be narrower. We can arrive at double."

"That's too much work."

"But I won't have to do it alone. I have you now. And if all goes well, we'll pull it all down, rebuild in brick. A small farm. You don't like it?"

"I don't know," I said.

He had killed Nero. There was no chance of turning back,

and it seemed he was making that offer of working together more for himself than for me.

I could hear Don Aniello Panzer's patter: "Draw up, ladies and gentlemen. Here you'll find all you need for your homes—scissors, corkscrews, pliers, all produced in the finest German factories."

I saw Gioacchino buying some candles. The stallholder wrapped them in brown paper, and he turned and moved in our direction. He caught my eye, but at the last moment he pretended not to know me and continued on.

un, Davide! Get out!"

I'd heard no footsteps in the corridor. My mother was at the door. She pushed it open, shouting.

"Run! He's going to kill you!"

If I had to record one memory of life with my mother, to choose just one, then this is it, without a doubt. The time when she tried to save me from the fury of her husband, Furtunà, my father, aspiring businessman in the pig trade.

Then I saw my father's arm at her neck, pulling her into the corridor. His great heavy bulk took the place previously occupied by the bony, gray-haired figure of my mother. He hadn't run as she had. He had let his anger swell to its maximum before he entered my room.

He was holding one of the handbills, one of the usual ones. At the center was a soldier with his right arm up, suffused by a white light that was supposed to be a symbol of his purity, while a dark purple toward the top of the sheet covered the darkness of the world.

"Read what's written here," he said.

"I can't read."

"They've all seen you going to that house again. Just remember, they have nothing to teach anyone. It's we who are giving them a patch of land to cultivate, and it's they who have to say thank you. And now read. I want to hear what they've taught you."

I took the handbill.

"Volunteer battalion, Mussolini's bersaglieri. Young men of Italy, join up. You'll be dispatched immediately to the front."

He snatched the paper from my hands. "And I'll tell you something else: If you go there again, you'll end up like that pig, the one you were so fond of."

I remained quite still when the first blow landed, just like Nicolas when I was beating him. My failure to react was an even greater affront. I seemed to be saying, Go on, hit me, you can't hurt me. As my father's arms crashed down on me, I remained with my face exposed to that torrent of abuse, of punches, of kicks. The shame he felt at having a son who went to Jews to learn to write must have been enormous. Unbearable. In his shoes I'd have done the same. In my shoes he would have done the same. Neither he nor I had any other choice. In terms of despair, in terms of feeling oppressed, my father and I were just the same.

Schiaffo, slap, written with two *f*s. In *vergogna*, shame, the *g* and the *n* together sound like a "nya." You don't say *scartellato*, humpbacked, but *claudicante*, lame. You write *zitto*, silent, with two *t*s.

We were entering a new phase, one in which soldiers take up arms and are dispatched to the front. The wailing of my mother and my sister could be heard behind the door. I remembered what Nicolas had said: They had no idea what they were running away from, what they had to defend themselves from.

By the time my father had finished, I could no longer feel my face. "That's how it's done," he seemed to be saying. Every blow reached its target. That would be enough, I thought, to show his friends that he had acted as every father should.

Yet in return, I was the one who felt stronger. My thoughts were being transformed into determination. When a person's body is exposed to the torturer, when that person knows he is right, the energy received is transformed. The energy is stored. I didn't realize this straightaway. It took me a couple of days or more, during which I walked around the whole village with my swollen face.

"Don't go out like that," my mother said.

I looked at my reflection in Signora Capogrossi the dressmaker's shopwindow. It will return to normal, I thought. My eyes lingered on the sign.

"Tailoring alterations undertaken."

I read it again, then spoke each word out loud.

Alterations. Undertaken. I could read.

hat have they done to you?" Gioacchino said when he opened the door. I recognized the smell of their kitchen, which I had substituted for that of our own. The table, the sink, the dull iron spoons, the cloths they laid over the dried plates to protect them from flies.

"First Nicolas, now you. This village is not as calm as it promises. I hope we haven't been the problem."

He sat me on the chair in the middle of the kitchen, like the village barber when he came to the house to cut our hair—my father's, mother's, sister's, mine—leaving a whole winter of hair on the floor.

He looked at my cheekbone, lips, eyes, and the great bruise on my forehead.

"I've been reading," I said.

"Well done. Now let's get you attended to. Certain things are more important."

He went to get some ointment. I didn't know where Nicolas was. His father hadn't called him when I arrived. It was generally the first thing he did. I wanted to show them the wounds I'd received because of their friendship. I wanted to tell Nicolas that we were even for what I'd done to him that night.

Gioacchino came back a few moments later with a jar and some bandages.

"No bandages," I said.

"The cuts must be disinfected. They can get worse. And then, you know, when you touch the wound, it becomes yours. The pain is transformed into a small strength. Things change, Davide, everything changes."

I never understood whether he was talking about the body or about something else. Whenever Gioacchino spoke, there was always a here and at the same time an elsewhere to which he was referring.

He unscrewed the lid, and a pungent smell came out.

"It's amazing you never use disinfectant. I sometimes think you live in another age."

"I'm a caveman," I said.

"Even cavemen used the leaves of medicinal plants."

"There's a tree with broad soft leaves. I use them after, with respect, after I've been to the toilet."

"Davide, please, I don't want to know about such things."

We both laughed.

"I'm pleased you haven't lost your sense of humor. Does it hurt?"

"It burns."

"I know it burns. When you buy it at the pharmacy, they always say that this one is new and doesn't burn, but it takes your breath away all the same. The good thing is that it lasts a second. I've always thought that wounds are like seeds from which plants germinate. We need to know what kind of plant we want to grow. What plant would you like?"

"I want a tree."

"Then you must plant it yourself. And I hope it doesn't have broad leaves."

We laughed again.

"Where is Nicolas?" I asked.

"I don't know. Teresa called earlier for him, then they disappeared. I thought you were with them."

I felt every wound all at once.

My whole skin was now burning.

Over the next few days neither Teresa nor Nicolas said anything about their meeting. I didn't mention it either and hoped it would come out during one of our conversations. More than once I thought I'd put too much weight on something of little importance. The material with which our friendship was made was becoming denser, more intricate, but I carried on taking my notebooks to the house at the end of the path. The private school, as I began to call it, was essential for the person I wanted to be.

Teresa said that I kept everything inside me, and only then did I manage to understand how deep that chasm in my breast really was.

Glass, *pasta*, *shoes*, *pears*, *fruit*, *wood*, *milk*. I filled pages with new words, those I saw in the windows of the village shops.

I had begun a slow reconstruction of Tora e Piccilli through writing. I stopped in front of a sign and read it aloud. I was no longer afraid of Furtunà and no longer cared that the villagers treated me as an idiot. I had never noticed until then how many words there were everywhere. There was as much writing to be found as there were rocks and trees, as the number of dogs living around Tora-Presenzano station, as the number of old people who spent their days sitting outside their houses. Inscriptions below the statues in church, shop signs, notices from the podesta, street names, surnames on doors. I memorized everything I read.

"Join the antiaircraft artillery."

"Germany is your true friend."

"Protect her! She could be your mother, your wife, your daughter."

"Don't snatch bread from our workers' children."

"Buy Italian products."

Fascist posters were my favorites. They were colorful and neatly designed. Some seemed like pictures on Nicolas's book covers, and even if the war was never shown, each image was infused with it. The dark colors in the background were brightened by distant lights, like the flash of an explosion. The faces of boys holding weapons were expressionless because the duty they were required to perform allowed no emotion, not even positive emotion. Love for the fatherland was above everything.

I had overtaken my sister Rosetta, but I was careful not to tell her that the word she had just uttered at the table wasn't used like that. Her notebooks were full of mistakes. She was a mediocre pupil with no ambition, just like her mother, whereas Furtunà and I wanted to make our way in the world, but followed two different paths. I kept silent at the table, and maybe they were also tired of me. The noise my family made with their mouths as they chewed was unbearable.

"NICOLAS DOESN'T FEEL WELL," GIOACCHINO SAID ONE day, when he saw me arrive. "This boy is always ill. When we were in Naples, we once spent ten days in the hospital. Could you help me make the soup, Davide? Do you mind?"

"All right," I said.

"You cut the vegetables. I'm making an apple cake, and even if there's nothing to celebrate today, it will be fine just the same. I couldn't find any cinnamon, so we'll have to manage without."

I did as he told me. I stayed in the kitchen and didn't ask to see Nicolas. Every now and then we heard his footsteps on the other side of the wall, and coughing. His weakness gave me some advantage over him, though I wouldn't have known how to use it.

A few days later, Nicolas started going out again. We went to the stream and fished with the lines he had managed to find at the farm. His voluble nature wasn't ideal for fishing, so we soon left the bank, and he asked me to show him the paths through the woods.

"We've been here before," he said after a while.

"Yes," I said.

"Woods are designed to make you lose your way."

"You need to find points of reference, then you can wander in and out whenever you want."

"Why are you letting me choose the way?"

"Because that's how you learn," I said.

"Then we're likely to be stuck here for days."

He kept repeating that if he were lost in the woods, he would never get out. He stopped and pointed to a large white rock.

"Come and get me here," he said. "You alone can manage to get here and back. It shows that you and I come from two different worlds."

I wasn't sure about what he had just said. He recognized my ability, but at the same time he was emphasizing how we would always be different.

Teresa also started seeing us again, though only on Sundays.

She spent the other days shut in her room studying. Nicolas and I waited for each Sunday to tell her about all the dangerous or idiotic things we had done.

Teresa sometimes laughed so much that she had to hold her stomach. Nicolas and I invented stories to amuse her. He also used his body as he talked, taking small steps forward or sideways, as though he were on a stage. I began to imitate him, trying out gestures that made them laugh. We worked well as a comedy duo on those days when our spectator was present, while on the other days we were shrouded in a veil of sadness.

I never asked him why Teresa had gone alone to see him that day, nor why neither of them had mentioned it. Nicolas was right. I was like one of those animals who could feel clouds gathering on the horizon, and my instinct told me that a storm was on its way.

A whole winter had passed since his arrival in the village. Every day, without fail, I looked to him for some confirmation of my progress. I was surprised how honestly and shamelessly I admitted my desire to imitate him at all costs.

In my father's world of manly vigor, the clumsy imitation of a Jewish boy who tended more toward art and meditation upon life was a grievous sin, and it led to the final rift with my family.

I collected as many words as I could during those rainy days when we couldn't see each other due to his ill health and his father's refusal to allow him out. The more words I knew, the wider and more understandable the world became. Nicolas discovered that the January coldness turned my hands red and covered my arms with blotches, and on wet days my lower teeth ached, and my mother gave me a cloth warmed on the fire that I held against my jaw. I didn't tell him that my mother prepared an ointment of oil and flour for the blotches on the skin and then recited some words that gave it a mysterious power.

Nicolas discovered the tyranny of coldness on the countryside and that every living being hidden in the woods had no other purpose than to survive the harshest weeks.

By the time February was over and the days were growing longer, I knew many more words. Meanwhile, Nicolas had lost weight and was irritable, like an animal born in freedom and now caged. With the first days of sunshine, we went out again. It was the end of March. The woods seemed to have been waiting for us.

TERESA BELONGED TO THE WOODS, LIKE ME. WE WALKED side by side, and among the millions of possible trajectories, our hands and arms sometimes happened to brush together. I wondered exactly what she felt.

One day, when we arrived at the farm, we found Nicolas in the fields, digging a furrow. He was pushing the spade down with his boot on the tread, loosening the ground by a few inches, then throwing the soil aside. I wasn't the only one acquiring new skills; he too was learning. His thinness was now nervous, his body seemed full of knots, and veins could be seen around his arms and neck.

When he saw us running toward him, he in turn ran off toward the woods, where he imagined he could hide or could lose us. He kept looking back to make sure we were following him.

I wanted to change the wind, to stop the movement of the earth or the gushing of the stream.

Teresa and I would never have been as fast as him. We both aspired to be like him, and to be him, but neither of us knew what he wanted. If he had asked us to leap from a tower, we'd have started to build the tower straightaway. All he asked of us in the meantime was to run.

THEN THE MEMORY OF THOSE MOMENTS BECOMES confused.

The images of that day that come to mind are those of a dream, in the cornfield, close to a bend in the stream. The grass was high, and we lay down in the middle of it. Our voices covered the sound of the leaves that rustled in the breeze.

"I want to go away," Nicolas said.

Teresa and I listened to these words with a slight pain in some undefinable part of the body. We didn't know what to say.

"Why?" she asked.

I gazed at the sky through the blades of grass that grew uniformly around my head. Those that bent obscured the view. Nicolas gave no reply, spoke about something else, and then the sound stopped, and we found ourselves immersed in a deep silence. The grass was damp. It seemed as if we were bathing in the stream. Then I got up and saw them, lying nearby with their mouths together in a kiss.

It's not that I had never thought about it. Teresa hadn't told me because certain things cannot be said. Secrets make you feel alive at first, but if you keep secrets for too long, they fester inside.

I stood up and started to run.

Everything about that day becomes distant, and the figure of Nicolas forms different shapes in my memories. No one can bring only good or only bad into the life of another. Every emotion, let run to its essence, leads to its opposite.

was taught to write by Jews, taught to read by Fascists, and taught to experience pain by Teresa. I was also taught that, without pain, words have no meaning. All that I learn from that moment is worth double.

I vowed never to return to Nicolas and his father's house, and I kept my promise. I continued to practice my writing, putting down all the words I knew in my notebook. As I was doing so, I saw my father talking to someone who had come about the pigs or to ask him to do some small job on his land.

I planned my days in the pigsty as productively as I could. I took with me all my father's Fascist leaflets and those distributed on Sunday mornings outside the church. No pigsty in the world had so much printed paper.

My father was proud of me. In people's eyes, I was becoming a good son, a good pig keeper, and a good Fascist.

I rebuilt two pens and set up a system to bring water to the animals without carrying it in buckets to the sty. Using some old tiles I built an irrigation channel that flowed downhill from the waterspout and into the pens.

With the scant light I managed to organize inside the sty, and with a poor library consisting of works of propaganda, I began to read and write by myself. But those words gave me no comfort. They were unvarnished words, exercises incapable of bearing the torment that I carried within. From all that I read I was looking for something that would speak to me.

I wrote on a sheet of paper: "The deep bosom of the ocean."

My body was no longer a part of me. It thrashed the animals that squealed and cried, while I cried with them. The pigs had never heard me shout. My voice frightened them. I ate little, lost weight, and my beard began to thicken. My skin seemed to grow pale with the long hours spent inside. The smell of my body became one with that of the pigs. I was transformed into the pig keeper the villagers imagined me to be, into the boy who has a special relationship with those animals because in the end he is no different from them.

OVER THE NEXT MONTHS I HEARD NO NEWS OF NICOLAS and Teresa. We lived nearby yet were far apart. I worked and studied in the pigsty. I read all I could lay my hands on, and the notebooks I had stolen at the market were crammed with phrases. I wasn't just copying down what I read but was now writing about unimportant events that happened during the day. "We sold a pig; Furtunà said we had made a loss after what they gave us." Or "Rosetta spent all day singing the song learned at church."

In the late afternoon I walked through the trees and took the path that went toward Teresa's house but stopped before the woods opened out. I couldn't remember such a long period of time without seeing her and thought I would soon forget her voice.

The summer was harsh and torrid. The heat was relentless during the day, and the mosquitoes at night made it hard to sleep. I felt better some days when I was less preoccupied with thoughts about Nicolas and Teresa, but on others I seemed always back at the same point.

I went with Furtunà to work on a neighbor's farm. It was better land than ours, better favored, better kept. The ground was always moist and aromatic and wasn't stony like our vegetable patch. When the job was done, we were given hens, olive oil, and a goat, as well as money that Furtunà kept in a drawer along with the rest.

In July, he and I began repairing the roof and the outside walls of our house, which we had been delaying throughout the winter. He explained that to repair a crack we had to drive an iron chisel into it, open it right up, just like cleaning a wound, and then waggle it about until the brittle part of the wall crumbled away. To build the new layer, we had to get back to the hard surface of the brick. We had only one ladder, and while he was on the roof I was working on the walls. Rosetta brought us glassfuls of water with squeezed lemon, which hurt my sun-cracked lips. She sat on a stone, watching and passing us tools when we called for them.

"Have you finished?" she asked now and then. Two of Furtunà's friends came one morning and told him Mussolini had been arrested. Furtunà heard the news from the roof. They carried on discussing what would happen, and when they left, he hurled his hammer at the trees, shouted something incomprehensible, and began beating himself around the head. Rosetta and I stood there watching as he hit what little hair he had with the palms of his hands, then struck his neck and his face. I seemed to see him alive for the first time.

ONE DAY TOWARD THE END OF SUMMER, I WENT WITH him to the village to sell a pig. The family who had bought it invited us into their yard.

"Bring it here," the man said. Then he turned to my father. "Have you heard, Furtunà? The girl is pregnant."

"Who?"

"Teresa, Glicine's daughter, pregnant with the Jewish boy who lives on Signora Ottavia's land."

"That girl never seemed quite normal to me," my father said. "If she were mine, I'd know what to do."

"I'm happy for them," I said. "New babies are always good news."

"Listen how well this young man talks."

I had changed the way I spoke, sounding more like Nicolas and his father than the people of Tora e Piccilli.

"Your son's grown quite big," the man said to my father. I imagined he was going to start inspecting my teeth.

My manner was no longer that of an awkward, timid young boy. I must have been less gawky. I noticed how the women of the village used to look at me.

We followed the man toward a corrugated metal hut. He opened what must have been the door.

"Put it in there," he said.

The pig dug in its heels and refused to go in.

So I took the stick and whipped its haunches until they were marked red. It started grunting and maybe crying.

I beat it harder.

"Get in! Get in!" I shouted.

The pig kicked in the air and looked for shelter between my legs. I heard it still crying. If only I could have cried too.

My father held my arm firm.

"Enough, enough. If we had to kill it, we'd have brought it here dead."

I stopped the beating.

"Have you gone mad? What came over you?"

"That's what I've become," I said.

I moved into the pigsty. The nights seemed endless. I slept with the pigs. I took the mattress and put it by the door. I did everything I could not to think about Nicolas and Teresa. My nightmares and preoccupations gradually became less insistent and began to fade, like the ghost stories I had heard as a child from my grandmother. She used to tell me that before you depart from this earth you linger here for several months, though no one can see you. Then, when your turn comes, you suddenly vanish, and only then can you say that you're dead.

Neither of them ever came looking for me. Maybe they too were expecting my ghost to go away from their lives.

One day I went to open the door for my mother and found her with a woman I already knew and a girl of about my age.

"This is Signora Lucia," my mother said. "And this is her daughter Immacolata. *Immaculate* like the Madonna. Look how beautiful she is. And if you knew how well-behaved."

"What do you want?" I asked, looking at the woman and the girl.

"You and Immacolata are growing up and need to start thinking about certain things." My mother paused for a moment before finishing. "You are two good young people and could make a fine family."

I looked at the girl. She kept her eyes down. Her hair was long and black, blacker than I had ever seen, and her face was as rough as the bark of trees that grow by the rocks. She seemed like a woodland animal.

"Signora Lucia has been gathering her wedding trousseau since she was ten. Everything: blankets, sheets, plates, cups."

I kept looking at the girl without catching her eye.

I wondered what her defect was, for it had to be an exchange on equal terms. They knew about my leg.

For a moment I glimpsed the possibility of leaving home.

"All right," I said. Then, just as the three women were going, I added: "Signora Lucia, the next time you come, bring me a Bible. Do you have one?"

She glanced at me for a few moments.

"We'll be back next week to talk to your father," she replied. "We'll bring it with us when we come."

I nodded goodbye and asked permission to go back and close the pigsty.

Signora Lucia returned the following week with her husband, Don Armando, and Immacolata, who wore a pink dress. I think it was supposed to allure me, or at least to show off her youthful looks, but never wear pink when the person you're about to meet spends all his time with pigs.

My mother had been to the village seamstress to have my Sunday trousers mended. My father explained how we had started going more often to market. We'd had more animals over the past year and intended to expand. Immacolata's father said something about a few rabbits they had reared at home, and our mothers exchanged stories about families in the village. Through the afternoon neither Immacolata nor I spoke a single word.

Before they left, Signora Lucia handed me the Bible I had requested.

IT WAS IN TINY PRINT. I READ IT BY RUNNING MY FINGER below each line and reciting the words quietly as if they were a prayer. I memorized whole passages in the hope they might be useful when I met Nicolas and Teresa. I was still doing everything for them. It was just as my grandmother had said: Their ghosts hadn't yet left me.

"Immacolata is a good girl. You ought to be pleased," my mother repeated.

I thought it must have been the same between her and Furtunà too—an exchange of prisoners, as apparently happened from time to time.

I had nothing against arranged marriages. That bond with no display of emotion and no prospect of failure was—I thought—an acceptable approach.

ne night I heard a knock at the pigsty door. I got up from my mattress.

"Davide, it's me. Open up, please."

It was Teresa.

"I knocked on the window of your room, and you weren't there. You could only be here."

"Why have you come?"

"You must help us. We need you."

"What do you want?"

"You have to help us."

I opened the door.

She stood before me like a ghost, white and skinny, so unlike the girl who worked at the ropeworks and came back from the seaside with her suntan marks.

From that day when I had seen her undress and dive into the water, I had found hidden and perhaps inexpressible desires in her, the same desires that dwelled in an unknown part of me. When I saw her kiss Nicolas, I had imagined she was pursuing the life that was rightfully hers and that this small demonstration of courage was no more than a declaration of war against her family and the whole village. She was rejecting the life she seemed destined to lead.

"Help us, Davide."

She took my hand.

"Who is it I have to help?" I asked.

"Nicolas . . . he's wounded. We must take him to the woods, to the old mill. We must hide him. Gioacchino and I can't do it alone."

"We won't even do it in three," I said. "I'll take the cart."

"The animal cart? All right, but please hurry. They're searching for him."

"Who are?"

"The Germans."

I opened the fence, trying to make no noise so as not to wake anyone in the house, and lifted out the cart.

"We won't take the path through the woods," Teresa said. "It's too dark. We'll get lost."

"No. I know the way. If you're hiding, then it's better we take that one."

I've always been afraid of the woods at night. It was Furtunà who told me you need to respect woodlands, mountains, streams, the land, rocks. As it grew dark, he used to say it was time to go home. Darkness distorts, trees change, and fear makes you reconstruct what you don't see.

As I pushed the empty cart, I told Teresa to stay behind me. We climbed the path that led to Nicolas's house, not knowing what I would find.

"Can you manage?" I asked.

"Yes," she replied, but I could hear her gasping for breath.

She couldn't keep up. The Teresa I had once known was always far ahead, and the person I had once been would have had to make do with second place.

"Keep up with me!" I yelled.

I didn't slow down, and when I had the strength, I tried to move faster.

"How much further?" Teresa asked.

"Not far," I replied.

"We're lost."

"I know the way."

"So why aren't we there yet?"

"I said I know the way. Just try to keep up with me."

After the last bend in the path, the woods opened out and we saw the lights of Nicolas's house in the distance.

We felt a temporary satisfaction, the wildlife fell silent, the upward slope leveled out, and we seemed dazzled by the faint light of the candle that Nicolas and his father kept in the kitchen.

A light was all we were looking for.

She went straight inside, while I hesitated.

I could hear Gioacchino's voice: "Where's Davide?"

"He's outside. We'll put Nicolas on the handcart and carry him on that," Teresa said.

"Good idea," he said. "Davide, come in. Where are you?"

I went inside.

I found them in Nicolas's room. Gioacchino was bent over him, wiping his leg with rags. Blood was still seeping from the wound. Nicolas was conscious and clutching at the sheets. When he saw me, he spoke my name and closed his eyes for a few moments.

"I was on the point of dying, and you didn't come to say goodbye," he murmured.

"It's just a graze," Gioacchino said. "He fainted from the pain, but he's all right now. Thank you for coming, Davide. Help me now to move him. We must lift him and put him on your cart. Teresa, you take his feet. Davide and I will take each side."

He had lost blood, and the medication was rudimentary. We lay him on the cart, moved his legs to his chest, into a position that would make him feel less vulnerable, the same position in which I always slept.

"That's fine," his father said, putting a blanket over him. "Now let's hurry."

"We'll cut through the woods," Teresa said. "Davide, you go ahead."

Nicolas weighed less than I thought. I was used to much heavier weights. Those months of work in the pigsty had made me stronger.

I didn't know why the Germans were searching for him. I wanted to take him where they had asked, and in this way to equal the score—now, after all they had given me, I could do something for them.

"Can you manage, Davide? Are we near?" Teresa asked.

"I can do it," I said. "Can you keep up? Are you tired?"

We crossed the hillock by the stream. I planted each leg firmly on the ground and pushed the cart step by step up the slope until we left the trees and found ourselves in open countryside. The outline of the old mill loomed in the distance.

When we arrived, we laid Nicolas on a wooden plank. His father lit an oil lamp for us. Someone must have spent the night there a long time before.

"We'll be fine here," said Gioacchino, putting his hand on his son's forehead to see whether it was hot. It was an instinctive gesture of concern that any parent would make. Nicolas had slept on and off through the journey.

"Let him sleep," Teresa said.

While Teresa and Gioacchino were making Nicolas comfortable on the bed, I went outside, back into the night. I was no part of the relationship that must have formed between the three of them. They may have had something to say that was not for my ears. Teresa joined me a few minutes later, having arranged the things they had brought from the house.

She came and stood beside me.

I recognized the gesture that Nicolas made with the cigarette before lighting it, tapping the tobacco to consolidate it, then putting it to his lips. It was the first time I had seen her smoke.

She held the smoke in her lungs, then slowly let it out.

"What happened to him?" I asked.

She paused, as if to reconstruct the events of the past hours. The smoke seeped from her mouth in the form of small clouds.

"A truck in the village was set on fire. Everyone's now frightened that there'll be a roundup. The Jews went and hid in the woods, Nicolas too, but some soldiers saw him running among the trees and took a shot at him. He managed to hide and came back for help."

We remained silent for a few moments, listening to the calls of the night animals. I could have identified them all. Teresa could have done so too. Just a few months ago she had said, "Did you hear that barn owl?" But now she stood smoking with her back against the wall of the derelict water mill. I could have asked how she was, could have said I knew about the baby, about how she and Nicolas had spent those months, and in this way could have found some new kind of understanding with them, but I didn't have the strength.

“Nicolas and his father were waiting for you,” Teresa said.

“You know why I didn’t come,” I said.

Teresa took a couple of steps back. She hugged her arms. Her body seemed to have no substance.

“The truth is we didn’t know how to tell you.”

“It’s no longer important. None of us is the same as before.”

She let her arms slip down to her sides.

“Everyone in the village knows, and you would have heard about it too. But no one knows I lost the child. I haven’t told Nicolas and Gioacchino yet. I don’t know how to tell even them.”

She stepped toward the darkness, then turned to look at me.

“It’s good it happened,” she said, gently shaking her head. “It’s a terrible thing to say, but I can say it only to you.”

“You have to tell Nicolas, not me.”

Teresa stubbed the cigarette out with her foot.

“Even though all that happened was my fault, I’d like to tell you I’m sorry,” she said.

I left Nicolas, his father, and Teresa at the mill and went back to the pigsty. As I pushed the empty cart, I seemed to see Nicolas still stretched out there. His image came and went intermittently, following the faint light that filtered through the branches.

Those months had left their mark upon our bodies. My feelings for Teresa were complicated and became more apparent as I gradually moved away from her. They needed distance and time to develop and intensify, like plants that grow with little water and little light. Teresa was too deeply rooted in me to enable me ever to break free from her.

The house that Immacolata would receive as a dowry had a kitchen overlooking a patch of wild ground, a bedroom, and a room that Signora Lucia called "the children's room," to her daughter's embarrassment. Signora Lucia was a frank woman who described things as she saw them.

Immacolata and I, on the few occasions we met, had barely exchanged a word. Nothing was right about the other, and from a certain point of view, that was all we had in common. We could start from there to create our relationship.

My father and I went to see the house. That morning we had a bath. My mother had filled the bathtub with hot water, going back and forth from the kitchen, and I kept my head underwater until I had no air.

During the visit, Immacolata and I were left alone in the children's room. "Do you like it?" she asked.

"I like it," I replied.

Even today I wonder how I found the strength to force out those words. I didn't want to hurt her.

I hated that house, and that room in particular. Nor did I like the mild, deferential character of Immacolata, so similar to that of my mother.

"Have you heard what's going on?" Signora Lucia said to Furtunà after a while. "If things don't settle down, we'll have no more peace."

"What's going on?" I asked.

But I knew what she was talking about. Everyone had begun to celebrate after September 8, thinking the war was over. But we now began to realize we had a different enemy, an enemy fighting within our own walls. We faced accusations of treason. The Germans came to Tora almost every day and took what they could find while the Jews in the area had hidden in the woods. Gioacchino decided to stay at home, for he felt sure no one in the village would betray him.

Signora Lucia seemed hesitant about what to say. Then my father spoke.

"Someone set fire to a German truck the other night. Now none of us know what might happen."

"Are they looking for Jews?" I asked.

"They don't know they're here. The local records have gone missing."

"Are the woods a safe place to hide?" Signora Lucia asked.

"No one knows," Furtunà said.

"And the old mill?" I asked.

My father looked at me, examining every muscle of my face, and understood that his answer was important. He shook his head. It wasn't safe.

"And what will happen if they find them and discover they are Jews?" I asked.

o one in Tora knew the woods better than I did. The days I spent in the darkness of the pigsty had accustomed me to seeing with very little light. I had become a being that, in Nicolas's words, was half man, half animal, able to get around in the densest areas. But that wasn't what I wanted to be. Nor was I the well-behaved son that Furtunà or my mother had wished for, though my father never told me what he wanted of me.

When I reached the mill, the candle was out. It was a wise precaution. I knocked at the door but there was no answer. I went in and moved toward the bed, where I had seen him on the last occasion. Suddenly I was thrown down. I found myself with my face against the wooden floor and could feel the blade of a knife at my back.

"It's good to receive a visit from you," Nicolas said.

"I've come to see if you're dead."

He sniffed my neck. "You've washed yourself for my funeral?"

He dropped the knife and rolled to one side.

I felt my rib cage re-expand.

"You frightened me to death," he said.

"I didn't bring you here on a cart to let you die just yet," I said.

"Why did you come? It's dangerous."

"Sooner or later, they'll be here. It's not safe. You must go somewhere else."

Nicolas lit a candle. I saw him walk. He managed to put weight on his leg.

"Davide, I need to thank you," he said.

"It's no longer safe here."

"I wasn't the one who set the truck on fire, though I wish I had."

"We have to go."

"Where?"

"There's a place in the woods, some caves. Only Teresa and I know them. They won't find you there. I'll tell your father, then Teresa can take him to see you. If you can manage to walk, we'll be there pretty soon."

"All right, let me collect my things, and we'll go."

While Nicolas put the food they had brought into a cloth, I picked up a book from the floor, opened a page, and began to read aloud. He stopped and listened closely.

Perhaps, more than worrying about his fate, I was more interested in showing him I could become like him.

WE STARTED WALKING. AT SEVERAL POINTS I HAD TO hold his hand to help him along or warn him away from thornbushes.

"If you left me here," he said, "I'd never get out of these woods. I'd be stuck here forever."

"Why should I do that?" I asked.

"For Teresa."

We stopped.

"I know you've spoken to her," he said, "and you knew she had lost the child before I did."

He waited for some reaction.

"We ought to have told you about it," he continued. "It was my fault, not hers."

"You didn't have to tell me."

"But this secret has moved us apart. And if I've been happy here at Tora, it's because I had you."

"We'd have moved apart even if you'd told me. That's the way things go."

"Teresa thinks so too. We can't protect everyone."

"She understands me," I said.

I looked ahead in the direction we were going.

"We'd better hurry."

We listened to the sound of our feet and our breathing. I made my way with a stick through the dense undergrowth along that rarely trodden path. My hands and arms were scratched. His must have been too. We had no more secrets, yet I thought how impossible it would be to go back to what we were before.

We arrived at the cave. It was a hole dug in the rock. When Teresa and I had found it, as children, we found traces of someone who must have spent some time there. Certainly someone who had run away. There were bottles, sheets of paper, bits of burned wood from a fire.

"They won't find you here," I said.

He looked at the cave.

"It's not very deep," I continued. "There are some rocks and wooden planks. Make yourself as comfortable as you can. I'll go and tell your father you're here."

"Will he know how to find me?"

"Teresa knows how to get here. He'll come with her. I must go. It will soon be light."

He moved toward me and held out his hand, waiting for me to shake it. It was hard for both of us to understand whether I was saving or deserting him.

"I'll go to your father," I repeated, then set off, leaving the woods behind, searching for the path that would lead me to Gioacchino's house. I stopped at every sound and tried to work out whether it was safe to continue in that direction.

Until I reached their house at last.

On the day of the engagement, we had lunch together at the house of Immacolata's parents, in a very large kitchen with a fireplace at the center. In the courtyard outside there were hens, and clothes hanging out on lines, and a small brown fox that allowed everyone to stroke it. You could smell the sugar-coated *graffette* that Immacolata's mother would serve at the end of the meal, and neighbors came in beforehand to offer their congratulations. A woman whom Immacolata called Zia Franca, but who was not a real aunt, gave her a rosary that she herself had taken to be blessed at the Church of the Madonna of Pompei.

The house had been cleaned from top to bottom, the curtains on the windows had been washed, and on a tray, covered by a fly net, were pieces of pork stuffed with raisins and pine nuts and tied with strings, ready to be cooked by Signora Lucia.

The other houses around the village would talk about our engagement as a small event that had broken up the monotonous sequence of days.

Immacolata's relatives had come from the nearby village,

and each kept telling me what a serious young man I seemed, complimenting my parents for the healthy education I'd been given. Over lunch, several toasts were drunk to me and Immacolata. Everyone stood and held their glasses high in our direction.

I couldn't wait for it all to end.

Even Furtunà, in his uncharacteristic intoxication, raised his glass to me. He too had changed that summer, like all of us, beginning from that day when I had watched him beat himself across his face on hearing of Mussolini's arrest. The news seemed to have come all at once: the Allied bombardment, Naples reduced to rubble, the stories of those hidden in the underground shelters, and the German plan to make scorched earth during their retreat. For him, war without faith was unbearable. He saw what had happened for the first time. The photo of the Duce was still in our kitchen next to the picture of Jesus, but now it was merely a photo that time would sweep away.

Immacolata's father came to speak to me when I went out to get some air.

"I've been talking to someone who works at the cement factory," he said. "Others from the village are already working there. There's a bus that goes each morning, and they're back at five thirty. In that way, you can spend some time with your family. They're looking for laborers, keen young men like you."

"I can't do much," I said.

"They'll tell you what has to be done. You don't need any schooling to work at a cement factory, and anyway it's nice. There are lots of youngsters. You can carry on working for your father until then."

They had thought of everything.

IN THE AFTERNOON WE WENT HOME. I CHANGED AND went to the pigsty. The animals looked pleased to see me back. Each of them greeted me from their own pen. I held out my hand, and each nuzzled it with their snout. I'd kept some food from the lunch and gave it to them.

When it grew dark, I went to the waterspout and found Teresa outside. She was sitting on the wooden bench made with slats left over from the construction of the fence.

I immediately thought of Nicolas in the caves and felt sure she was there for something to do with him.

"How long have you been here? Why didn't you knock?" I asked.

"I've only just arrived. I was resting."

She held out a small package. "It's something for you."

"I don't want any presents," I said.

She kept her hand out, waiting for me to take the package, but seemed to find it hard to keep her arm straight. I watched her hand open and the package fall to the ground. She looked at me for a moment, rolled her eyes back, and fainted.

I leaned over and called her name. I stroked her face, but there was no reaction. I bent down and took her in my arms. When I felt her body for the first time, I was astonished how little she weighed. It was exactly the weight I had imagined in my fantasies.

I carried her into the pigsty and laid her on the mattress. I touched her face again with my open hand, felt the firmness of her cheekbones and the soft flesh immediately below. I put a blanket around her and held her hand, hoping to figure out how serious her condition might be. If she hadn't opened her eyes in the next few moments, I would have called for help at the pharmacy. But Teresa responded to the touch of my hand, squeezing it at regular intervals as if she were having contractions. Her eyes were open, though I wasn't quite sure what they were looking at. I touched her face again. I first ran my finger over her forehead, then traced around the perimeter of her eyes. Teresa closed them as it passed. Her skin seemed to relax.

"How do you feel?" I asked.

"I'm fine," she replied with her eyes closed.

I studied the small green veins of her neck and the archipelago of tiny ones that I knew from memory. She continued to squeeze my hand at intervals, like a pulsation. I moved my mouth to her ear to ask again how she was, and when I was close to her, she turned toward me with her eyes still closed and kissed me on the mouth. I felt her breath and her tongue. It was the first time I had kissed a girl. I was sitting beside her as she lay flat, and I remained perfectly still so that it would last as long as possible.

Teresa held out her arm and put it behind my head. Her gentle pressure was enough for me to understand she wanted me to climb on top of her.

Eagerly I kissed her open mouth. I felt the warmth of her breath. I undid my trousers, and she took off her underpants and encircled me with her legs.

I don't know how long we remained in that position. We fell asleep, not moving. During my brief moments of wakefulness, I watched her sleep. It was impossible to know what changes that night would bring, but those few more minutes of sleep that she granted me were all I possessed. Her eyelids moved rapidly, and I thought this must be the speed of her dreams.

AT FIRST LIGHT, THERE WAS A SOUND OF BANGING AT the door.

"What is it?" Teresa asked. She sat up. The sudden noise had frightened her.

"Stay here. Don't let anyone see you," I said.

"Davide, open up." It was the voice of Gioacchino.

I covered myself with the blanket and went to the door.

Gioacchino had the face of someone who had just lost everything. In his hands he was clutching his small metal glasses, which looked like a metal insect in the faint morning light.

"Nicolas is not at the cave any longer. The Germans went into the wood taking the path by the stream. If they followed that route, I knew they'd get to his hiding place. So I waited, and when I saw them come back, I ran straight there, but the cave was empty."

He was a few feet away, looking as if I might tell him what had happened. Then, when I said nothing, he left. I turned and looked back inside the pigsty. Teresa was sitting on the mattress, completely naked. She had heard it all and was staring at me.

Part Two

THE DEEP BOSOM OF THE OCEAN

 fled to Naples, hidden in Don Aniello Panzer's truck, on the day after Teresa and I had learned that Nicolas was no longer in the cave. We had no idea whether he had run away or been arrested. All the same, the blame for what had happened was marked with our names.

I went off without saying a word to my family or to Immacolata. I had little money in my pocket. When Don Aniello Panzer closed the hatch and found me sitting huddled among buckets and broom handles with my knees to my chest, he understood straightaway that I was escaping.

"Who's looking for you?" he asked.

"I need a lift," I said.

"Listen, if the Germans stop me, you must swear I knew nothing about it."

"Do they ever say anything? Don't they let you through?"

"There's nothing that can't be bartered for something I have on the truck. Maybe even for someone who's trying to escape. So be sure to keep quiet."

"All right," I said.

"I'll take you to Naples, to the station. I'll stop there at the back, and when I open the hatch, you vanish without a word."

I could still smell Teresa on me. When she rose naked from the bed and gathered her clothes, my last image was of a barely perceptible tremor that ran across her lips: one of the underground earthquakes that she herself had spoken of, when the lava that flows beneath the earth's surface gets hotter and its energy cleaves the ground into ravines and precipices.

I fell straight asleep.

MEMORIES OF MY EARLY DAYS IN NAPLES ARE BLURRED. The American jeeps. Children with bare feet. An air of celebration and defeat. Bombed-out buildings. Whole families left to live in those shelters that Nicolas had told me about after their homes had been destroyed. Large delousing syringes that sprayed white DDT powder against typhus. Flour and everything else that could be stolen from the American Liberty ships and sold on the black market, including parachutes whose silk was used for sewing wedding dresses. Americans who were liberators and at the same time the new masters of what was left. Neapolitans who had freed themselves from the Germans by all possible means, sacrificing the lives of children they called *scugnizzi*, street kids.

I slept at the central station, crammed together with others who lived there permanently, sheltering under a metal roof along with a colony of pigeons. It seemed impossible to imagine how people, however poor, could survive without a home. It was a different poverty from what I had known until then. There were people at Tora e Piccilli with no land and no animals, but these had nothing; they had no one. In Furtunà's house I had a roof, a bed, and food to eat, and I had pigs that respected me because they knew I was the master. At Naples station, I was master of nothing.

On the platforms, we were a small army in search of food and clothing, and those more familiar with the city knew how to find them. The rules were the same as those that governed the woods around Tora: Be quick, be discreet, and keep a tight hold on the small area you're able to control.

In the early days I saw Nicolas and Teresa everywhere among those who had just stepped off the train or were entering bars. I felt sure they would come looking for me, and I sometimes heard their voices among the crowd, calling my name. I once mistook a girl walking hand in hand with her mother for Rosetta, and went up to her, forcing her to hide in the woman's breast. Another time I thought I saw Teresa hurrying toward me, scared by all those people. They would come to find me. I felt sure of it.

Boys younger than me were living in the station. The war had torn many families apart, and life had become a matter of everyone for themselves. They moved around in groups and gave each other nicknames I didn't understand. They were cunning and quick, disappeared all day and returned at night with what they had managed to steal. I wished I was one of them, but I wasn't so smart, nor did I know the streets around the station like they did. If I wanted to remain there, they said, I'd have to move to the far platforms, those away from the passengers.

It was hard at that time even to find cardboard to lay on the ground, and whatever you had was stolen. I ate in a church on Via Marina where the nuns prepared warm food. Vegetable broths, overcooked pasta, rotten fruit, and stale bread were what those waiting their turn in the queue had to look forward to. They let you into enormous bombed-out rooms. You ate with the taste of bare stone in your mouth. The city water supply didn't work, and we each had a single cup of water. After you had eaten, you were allowed to use the toilet but had to make way immediately for someone else.

One day, as I was waiting my turn, I heard they were looking for people to unload boxes in a small warehouse not far from there. I had to continue straight down the road without turning. So I left the station, heading toward what I discovered to be the eastern part of the city.

As I walked along the road that ran parallel to the sea, I saw many large buildings reduced to rubble. There had been a bomb blast near the post office not long before. The rooms of houses still standing were open to the view of passersby, like people forced to strip in public. A kitchen, a bedroom, a bathroom with blasted tiles.

I found a job in a small soap factory at San Giovanni a Teduccio. When he saw me, the foreman said he couldn't take a cripple.

"I can unload boxes," I said.

"Who sent you? Who do you know?"

"No one. They told me there was work here."

"We can't just take anyone."

"If you've taken these, then you can take me too," I said, pointing at the men working in the yard.

The foreman approached. "How dare you? They, at least, can walk properly. Anyway, show me, take that box, load it on the truck."

The other workers stopped to watch what was obviously a test.

"Go on, *ciunco*, cripple!" one of them shouted.

"Get out of here!" another shouted.

I lifted the box, not letting a single piece of soap fall. The boxes were no heavier than the water buckets for the pigsty, or the buckets full of animal mash, or the dead pig that my father and I lifted onto the cart.

"I don't know," the man said. "It's one thing to carry one box, but it's another to carry them all day. This is no job for you."

I moved up closer. He had a notebook with the names of workers, days, and working hours.

"I can write. I'm just at the start, but I can write," I said.

"But *se tu nun sai parlà nemmeno 'o nnapulitano*, if you can't even speak Neapolitan."

"I'll show you," I said.

He handed me the paper.

"Write: Deliver eight boxes to shop in Via Foria opposite botanic garden."

"Do I have to write in Italian or in Neapolitan?" I asked.

"Just get on with it!"

The foreman's writing was a mess. It sloped to one side, perhaps because he wrote quickly or because he had nothing firm to rest the paper on. Keep your wrist firm, Gioacchino would say. Move your pen and not your arm. The fingers write the letter, the wrist moves on to the next one. It's a dance in which each plays its part. When the word appears, then the object exists. If you write badly, the objects appear badly. So you must take care over each one. That's what he would have said.

There were no lines on the page. It was blank. I had no points of reference. I began writing down what he had told me. I had never written the word *botanic*. I didn't know what it meant. It was just a sound that I had to represent with the right letters. Those who had watched the test of strength hadn't yet gone, nor was it apparent whether they were siding with me or with the foreman.

"Have a look," I said, handing him the paper.

He read it to himself.

"Come on, *guagliú*. Come on, boys. Back to work. Leave the new bookkeeper alone. When you've finished loading, he'll tell you where to deliver." Then he turned to me. "What's your name?"

"Davide."

"Listen here, Davide. I can give you less than what these who load the trucks get paid. They break their backs, and you'll be sitting about. And you've seen what they're like. They won't take it kindly if they hear you're getting the same day rate as them. What do you want to do? Do you want to stay?"

"I want to stay."

"I'll show you the storeroom. The boxes on the floor need to be counted by the type of soap, then you write it all down in this register. Then we can tidy up the goods. Count the blocks eaten by mice on the other page, they go to the nuns. Those with American writing, you mustn't count them because they mustn't appear anywhere."

The warehouse had a sickly odor because of the rat poison they kept spraying. The smell of soap sometimes reminded me of Teresa's mouth and her neck.

"Take nine boxes and put them into three piles."

"But you said I wasn't to move the boxes."

"Don't worry," he said, "just take them."

"Those?" I asked, pointing at some.

"Those."

I took the nine boxes and stacked them.

"This is where you work, bookkeeper. This is your desk. How about that?"

It occurred to me a few days later that I had started doing just the same as Teresa was doing at her father's ropeworks. I recorded what came in and what went out, what the workers had damaged during transport, what the rats had nibbled. And when the accounts didn't balance, it meant only one thing, that the workers had made a few boxes vanish so that they could sell a few blocks of soap. They called the man who had done the job before me "the bookkeeper," so having inherited the job, I also inherited the name.

Those who loaded the trucks would pick on me. Each time I went off they would take the boxes of the desk and load them onto the truck, or they'd draw rude pictures on the paper I was writing on, and in block capitals, in juvenile handwriting, I'd find the words "A GIFFT FOR THU BOOKKEEPPER."

I wished Teresa and my father knew I had a job in Naples and that I had a desk made of nine boxes of soap. I imagined how the news might already have reached Tora and how Furtunà was admitting he'd been wrong about me. It was an absurd idea that plagued me for several weeks before it faded into the darkness from which it came.

The queue on payday was more exhausting than a whole day of loading and unloading. The foreman and I kept a record of what had been damaged during work. Cardboard boxes were split, soap fell out, and the boxes became unusable. The broken box was deducted from the worker's pay. Sometimes they tried to scare me.

"Bookkeeper, if you mark this box down I'll kill you."

If the foreman wasn't there, I didn't mark it down.

Some of the better-off families in the district would sell some of the food they cooked for a small price. You could sit and eat at their table. Each home found its own way of making money. I used to go to a family who lived in a *basso*, a ground-floor room open to the street, behind the church of the patron saint, and I'd sit with children who were quite used to having a stranger at their table. I looked at their thin faces and listened to their chewing. The mother would sometimes give me something to take with me for the night. When one of the children was absent from the table, it meant I was eating their meal.

I discovered that the sea was close by. You had to cross a line of buildings and some railway tracks. The sand wasn't like it was in those stories Teresa had told me about her summers. It wasn't soft and golden, but wild and inhospitable, black and scalding, even at night.

"It's the sand that comes from Vesuvius," they said, pointing to the volcano that seemed so close.

I followed some men who worked at the factory, took a large piece of cardboard from the storeroom and a rag to use as a cushion, and made up a bed beside them. There were some old, abandoned warehouses that gave shelter, even if the wind never stopped. At dawn you would hear the colony of gulls attracted by the boats hauling in the nets. The competition for food with the fishermen was ferocious: The birds swooped down, folded their wings—transforming themselves into arrows—controlled their trajectory with precision, and snapped up the morsel they had in sight, clasping it in their beak.

Nicolas had told me about the deep bosom of the ocean, Teresa had described the sand, but they hadn't told me about the waves. Waves are impossible to imagine. A rough sea is impossible to imagine. The endless sound of the sea crashing onto the beach is impossible to imagine. My teachers were far from perfect.

In the darkness of the night, I watched the white line of foam shine and break against the sand. The wind brought droplets of brine up to where I was sheltering. With that continual sound, like breathing, I was able to sleep and seemed still to hear Teresa's breath as she clasped me between her legs, to feel the energy with which she pulled me toward her, her open mouth, the redness of her palate, the whiteness of her teeth.

At the factory they started calling me cripple, humpback, bandy-leg, but they meant turncoat, traitor. They thought I wanted to put on a show in the hope the foreman would treat me favorably. When I was out of sight, they would walk about dragging their legs and aping my dialect, just as they had done in my village many years before.

I was learning new words all the time. I was writing out addresses without knowing where they were. The dark side of Naples began to emerge thanks to place-names that suggested narrow passageways: Vico Lammatari, Vico Paradisiello, Vico Purgatorio ad Arco, Vico Tutti i Santi. They were words that evoked subterranean worlds and stairways to paradise. The street names conjured an idea of a city full of secrets, of corners steeped in prayer or magical charm.

In the meantime, my first winter in Naples had ended. One day the foreman brought a pair of shoes he no longer wore, letting me have them without the others seeing.

"Don't tell anyone," he said.

When there was a drop in work, he told the workers that two of them would have no job the following week.

"It's not my fault," he added.

He gave them the chance to get together and choose among themselves. They had two days to give him the names.

That same evening, I asked for my last week's wages and left the job.

I counted the money I had and slept for the last time in the place where I'd been staying, listening to the waves. That sound had become familiar, and after my last night on the beach I headed for the city center, along Corso San Giovanni and Via Marina, wearing my new shoes that had meanwhile become familiar. There were American jeeps along the road. The soldiers smoked and talked loudly in a language they mixed with the few words they'd learned in the Neapolitan dialect.

"*Guagliò*, boy!" some kid from Ohio shouted. There were young boys around nearly every vehicle, holding their hands out for chocolate, candies, or gum to chew. They would run off after they received them, shouting insults in dialect about the soldiers' mothers. The Americans, on the other hand, were looking for women. It cost little to have a *segnorina*. In some passageways it was the main activity, and whole families depended on it for their survival. Nobody would turn down American dollars or Allied Military lire. Nobody would refuse clothing, cigarettes, or food. Everyone wanted currency to spend on the black market. All of Naples was for sale.

The Germans bombed the city in mid-March. Their planes were called Junkers Ju 88s. I felt the ground open and quake. A few days later, a column of smoke blotted out the sun: Vesuvius had erupted. Old folks would complain it wasn't fair that the people of Naples should always suffer: "The dog always bites the hobo," they used to say, referring to themselves.

I began to learn my way around the city, understanding its layout and how some districts were so vast and densely populated that they were a city within a city. Corso Garibaldi, the Rettifilo, Via Toledo, Via Marina, Via dei Tribunali. I learned the names of churches and hospitals, which were points of reference for all directions, since Neapolitans always recognized authority. They deferred to anyone in uniform, whether military, ecclesiastical, or medical. In every alley there was a shrine—*'a Marunnella* they called it—a small statue of the Madonna to whom the inhabitants of that alley turned. She kept a mental list of the sinners and the virtuous, and she always knew the right thing to do.

uring those earlier years I tried to hold within me that powerful feeling that had kept me bound to Nicolas and to Teresa. They were more essential to me now than then, for they defined what I wanted to be, they were the reason why I had left, and they were the only possible motive for my return. Thorns sometimes hurt only when you try to pull them out of the flesh. Well, my thorn carried two names.

I found a job at a vinegar factory and tried immediately to get on good terms with the other workers. I made friends with them and managed to do so by secretly siding with them against the boss, as they all did. When I told the owner I had worked as a bookkeeper and could keep a storeroom in order, he replied that in that factory of his there was nothing to keep in order and the only work to be done was filling bottles, cleaning out vats and distillery equipment, preparing bottle tops, and putting the bottles into boxes. It was the owner himself who told me the most important thing was to get used to the smell of vinegar.

"Breathe it in," he said. "This is a smell you'll never get rid of."

I breathed it in. He could never have slept in a pigsty.

I rented a room in Via Santa Chiara, not far from the vinegar factory. The bathroom was on the landing, behind a curtain, shared with the other rooms. I tried to use it only at night while the others were asleep. Mine was not a real room, just a small space with a window, where they had once kept cleaning mops and buckets.

On Sunday mornings, in springtime, I went to watch the first communions along the street where I lived. The little boys wore monastic robes and held a candle with a blue silk bow while the girls carried a basket with a gift to leave on the altar: *salame*, *caciotta* cheese, jars of sliced eggplant in oil. The poorest families gave out sugared almonds to passersby.

The streets in the old center were no more than alleyways, and some were so narrow that by stretching your arms you could touch both sides. No one noticed me, even though I was new to the area. In the center of Naples, you could spend your whole life as a stranger or be treated by the whole district like their own son. It was up to you.

The room I had taken was empty, without even a base for the mattress. The woman who rented it got her son to give me some wooden planks. I would have been comfortable with just a blanket.

"This is a rough place for an outsider like you, and you're so young," she said as I handed her the first money.

"You needn't worry," I answered.

I slept on the floor, wrapped in rags and cardboard as I had done on the beach, but it was better here because I had a door to shut behind me, and the feeling of safety for the first time in a long while made me sleep the whole night. Such a deep sleep brought a respite from the whirl of thoughts around Nicolas and Teresa. I was kept safe by that drafty wooden door and by the little picture of San Gennaro wedged into the lock and by the metal handle.

The owner's name was Concetta. The locals called her Cuncè. She had other apartments along the same street, and from her house she sold whatever she could get—clothing, food, cigarettes—like everyone else. When I came back from the vinegar factory, her son and I did small errands for her. I received nothing in return, but showing that I was a friend of Cuncè meant that I was recognized and protected. On Sundays, she would bring me something cooked, half a plate of pasta, a couple of rissoles made with bread, parsley, and garlic. People in the district had different things to say about her—that she helped those in need but also that she lent money with interest.

Each day I bought enough to eat, and what wasn't legally available could be found on the black market, a trade carried on from house to house, door to door.

The first thing I did was to learn Neapolitan. If I couldn't get by in its language, the city would remain out of reach. No one spoke Italian in the district where I lived or in the vinegar factory. When I said something in my own village dialect, they laughed and called me a peasant, a yokel.

There were words I had never heard before, like *sanzaro*, mediator; *schiattamuorto*, undertaker; or *chianchiere*, butcher. There were a thousand insults in constant use, like *sfaccimma*, sperm; *lota*, slimy; *strunzo*, shit; *chitemmuort*, may your family rot in hell; *curnuto*, cuckold. People alternated between *my friend* and *cumpagno mio*. At some bars you could pay for drinks in dollars. *Money* and *sòrde* were essential words.

The monotony of each day enabled me to pass the months painlessly until they began so much to resemble each other that they overlapped. Minor events occasionally moved the single mass of time. Through the window I used to watch a girl assistant in the shop opposite the vinegar factory. For a short while, my thoughts about her and about Teresa ran side by side until at times I confused the two, but when her job came to an end, I stopped looking across in her direction.

I caught a fever and my body, which until that moment had never failed me, succumbed. Cuncè found me in my room, for which she still had the key. I was lying on the bed, sweating, my face white. She took care of me, putting damp cloths on my forehead, and brought me food.

One Sunday morning I went to Mergellina. It was the area that Nicolas had told me about, the place where he and his family had lived, where he had been to school and had acted in the theater.

I asked whether anyone knew Nicolas or his family and eventually found a man who nodded eagerly. Of course he knew them—Gioacchino, Nicolas, his sisters, his mother.

I wanted to kiss that stranger's hands. I hadn't made it all up. Nicolas really had been there in the world before we met.

"None of that family is here any longer. I heard the mother and daughters had gone to relatives in the north. No one knows where. They were well liked in the district."

ONE EVENING A WEEK I WENT INTO A HOUSE THAT HAD girls. I'd go with one of them, never the same. I didn't choose, I accepted the first one who came up to me, even if she was much older, even if I didn't like her. It didn't take long for me to overcome my fear. I was afraid they'd judge me by my leg or by the smell of vinegar. I'd lie on top of a girl I didn't know for a few minutes in an airless room where I was asked to wash my private parts in the washbasin of a tiny bathroom. I discovered that the moment of pleasure was followed by a feeling of emptiness and weakness. I hated the urge that made me visit those girls. I could feel it stirring midweek, a fixed moment determined by something that was me, but which at the same time was not a part of me. Immediately after the sex I saw things as they were: a fetid room, a washbasin in the bathroom that dripped, a fat woman whose mouth stank of cigarettes. She turned me out as soon as I had finished because she knew how I saw her. The truth was unbearable for me and for her. Then I would take a walk, breathe in the air, and stop to eat fried pizza in a *basso* or, if it was Sunday, there'd always be someone roasting artichokes or ears of corn, as Furtunà used to do.

IT WAS CUNCÈ WHO TOLD ME THE WAR WAS OVER. SHE came knocking at my door with a slice of Neapolitan *babà*, a soft cake soaked in liquor she had prepared for her son's birthday.

"I managed to find some rum," she said. "Eat slowly—you're not used to it—or else you'll get drunk. Today we can celebrate twice." I felt the alcohol spread over my palate, making my head spin. Then she added: "I know you go to the girls every now and then. There's nothing wrong with that. You're a man, but you're the kind of man who needs a wife."

I wondered what change the end of the war would bring. I always felt I had been watching from a distance—when I was at Tora e Piccilli as well as after my move to Naples. It had now ended, but I didn't know exactly what had ended.

"You're old enough to start looking around, Davide. No offense, you're a good boy; people will get used to your leg. Come, eat some more *babà*. Today's an important day. It really is. I thought I'd never live to see it."

The change was something difficult to feel, but all I could do was breathe it, like the air.

ne evening, on my way back from the house where the girls lived, walking along Via Toledo toward Piazza del Gesù, I saw a shop with its shutters up. People were sitting inside on what looked like a small stage made from several wooden sections and surrounded by black painted panels. Each of them was reading from a sheet of paper they had on their lap, making corrections, or drawing signs around the margins. It seemed at first as if each was writing independently, but these were the speeches of a play whose plot was gradually rewritten as the reading progressed. The characters followed different paths but were moved by the same desire.

I wasn't the only spectator. Grouped along the walls were a handful of men who, like me, had nowhere else to go. We were protected by the darkness of the room, and those phrases reached us like the waves of the sea as you watch them from the shore. Listening to those slow, measured, persuasive voices, I felt a kind of peace for the first time since I had left Tora.

I discovered that the Dictionary of Insects, as the company was called, met twice a week at no fixed time, moving the days according to need. I don't know how they exchanged information, but the rehearsal room was near to where I lived, and I could pass each evening to check. What a strange thrill I felt when I found the shutters up.

The actors' parts became familiar to me, and sometimes, when I was at work, in a moment of distraction, I would come out with one of their lines. The owner of the vinegar factory would turn to me, then put his finger to his temple to indicate there was something not quite right with my brain. Those words were unlike all the others: They came from the same place as the deep bosom of the ocean.

I was amazed by the changes the actors made each week to the script, a continual development that was quite unlike the theater I had imagined, where a character's role was fixed forever. I had never been to see a play but had imagined it performed in exactly this furtive and undercover manner. Nicolas had been the only one to tell me about it, and like everything about him, it was impenetrable and illicit.

Apart from the voices of the actors, the most important thing was the darkness. Sometimes they rehearsed with a lamp that shone toward them. There were several seconds of total darkness before the lamp was switched on, and that seemed like the light of the world, from which everything had begun.

THERE WAS A MAN CALLED FERDINANDO WHO COORDInated the others and arranged the rehearsal times. He wasn't a director because he didn't give instructions, except for when they had to move from one scene to another. I began calling the actors woodsmen because I thought that was where the play was set, but then one evening they were rehearsing the part of somebody who was shipwrecked, where the tide was sweeping him away. I wasn't too far wrong since there was a certain similarity between woodland and open sea.

One evening there was an empty seat among the actors, and they asked me to fill it. I had to read the script they had put on the seat, otherwise they couldn't go ahead.

"Can you manage it?" Ferdinando asked. "You come here every evening. You'll know the lines by heart. But only if you want to."

"I'm not too good at reading," I said.

The others looked at me as though I'd said something stupid. I didn't feel embarrassed or awkward. It was a truth that I could admit with no sense of shame. "I'm not too good at reading" was a phrase that could be in one of their parts. I had already started to perform.

"Just try. We'll listen," Ferdinando said.

This was my first small step toward the stage. I felt the force of attraction emitted by a chair that was looking for an occupant. Before I began, I looked at the chair in which I had been sitting among the audience, and I looked at the others taking part in the rehearsal. I wondered why Ferdinando had chosen me, then took hold of the script. A girl found the exact line and pointed it out. "You have to start from here and finish there," she said quietly.

I started reading the part, following the directions that were given to me—too slow, too fast—and then more naturally, for I knew the whole play and my memory took over from my reading. After the few lines I had recited, I felt part of that group in a way that even today I cannot describe in any other way. That group of strangers had accepted me as one of them.

"You did well," Ferdinando told me as we said goodbye. He took a last drag on his cigarette. "Come back the day after tomorrow."

"And the one who plays that part?" I asked.

"He said he won't be coming anymore," and he stubbed out the butt with his shoe.

I couldn't sleep that night. The next day seemed interminable. I was excited but, with no chance of telling Nicolas and Teresa about the part I'd been given, my excitement was mixed with long spells of anxiety.

Only later would I discover that it was a fundamental condition of acting that I had to gradually vanish as a person. Being nothing enabled me to perform everything. Nicolas had never explained that disappearance was essential.

FERDINANDO WAS THIN AND LANKY, WORE HIGH-NECK sweaters, and always held a cigarette between his thin, nervous fingers. It was his distinguishing feature. His face was pockmarked, as if he'd survived a machine-gun attack. He resembled every building in Naples, except that he seemed proud of it. The confidence with which he moved and talked attracted the women of the company. His good looks were unlike those of Nicolas, legitimated by the admiration of those around him. Nicolas was a unique example of his kind, whereas Ferdinando was a natural leader who felt he shouldered the destiny of the group.

"Ours is not a traditional theater company. Each person writes their own part in the play. The characters find a natural path, and decide for themselves. One day we will go beyond the script, but at this moment we're not yet ready. There's no place for vanity. Actors are ordinary workers, the medium through which theater develops. We want to take our writing to different places, to unlikely surroundings. We're interested in places where people meet. We want audiences to be part of a performance, not to feel they are spectators. This city is still half-derelict; we want to perform on the rubble. We're different from Eduardo De Filippo. We're telling the story of a city that doesn't yet exist, but will exist. We are new. We are free."

Those words exploded in my mind. The city that until then had allowed me only a subterranean life was beginning to emerge between the walls of that tiny theater.

"Give him a break from your chatter," Claudia said. She was dark-haired, thin, and had a small dark patch on her neck. They lived together. Everyone knew, though it certainly wasn't obvious. Their respectability made everything purer, and purity was the basis of Ferdinando's theater.

We were in the rehearsal room, they had brought things to eat, and some drank directly from the bottle.

"I think Davide should know what our idea is. We have a manifesto. We all took part in writing it. It's what we are."

"And you, Davide, what do you think?" Claudia asked.

"I don't know enough about it," I stammered.

"But you'll have some idea, won't you? Do you think the old will be replaced by the new, or is the old the only way ahead?" Ferdinando asked.

"The theater, you mean?"

"It's the same for everything."

"I think true things will last in the end. Truth doesn't belong to old or new. It's the same for everything."

"But yet, no, the new is unstoppable. It will take over everything: us, them, the whole lot."

Ambitious, foolish, brave. Ferdinando's words had been tried and tested against more competent adversaries. The bolder they were, the more Claudia was drawn to them. I felt it clearly. Ferdinando did what wolves always do—he was continually showing he wasn't afraid, and above all that he could keep the newcomer at bay. It was my first real lesson in theater.

On my way home I stopped in the alley where the girls were. It was late but the door wasn't yet shut. I felt so excited that it seemed impossible to go to sleep. I knew that Ferdinando would consume his frenzy on Claudia, while I would have to pay for mine.

"Oh, it's you," said the woman who was always there to greet me. "Who shall I call down? They're all asleep."

"Forget it, I don't want to wake anyone. I'll go, it's better."

"There's Marilina, she likes you. I shouldn't tell you, but there are certain things I know. She'll get up if I ask her."

"Wake someone else then, not her."

"Marilina is the prettiest."

"Not her. I've never liked her. Wake someone else who doesn't like me."

The woman went to the inner rooms and came back a few minutes later.

"Go to Ornella in the third room."

"Oh my love," Ornella said, when I entered, "but what a time to arrive."

I couldn't see who it was. She had a pillow on her face to shade the light from the corridor.

"Isn't it late?" she said.

She slipped off her underpants, still covering her face with the pillow.

"I'm nobody's love," I said, climbing into her bed. I lay on top of her and pushed hard against her pelvis. She kept still, accustomed to thrusts of another weight, to bodies twice as heavy as mine.

Once I was back home, I took a piece of paper and started noting down the changes to the part I would read the following week. I had never written anything more than a page, but the words kept flowing. For my whole life I'd been carrying them with me, and for my whole life I'd been waiting to put them down in writing. By the time I had finished, it was light outside.

ON THE NEXT OCCASION I WAS NERVOUS, TREMBLING. Ferdinando nodded that it was my turn. I had learned the words by heart and could look away from the paper as I read. This enabled me to take long pauses, to move my hands, to look at the others, to gather information about what was happening around me, to look out at the audience along the walls. It was an advantage. I let the words cross through my body and let my throat reshape them without ever losing control over them.

My monologue was the shortest, the most imprecise, the worst of those heard that evening, but Ferdinando and Claudia started to view me with different eyes. I couldn't say exactly what had changed in them, or in me, from then on.

"Where do you come from?" Claudia asked when we were alone.

"I don't think you'll have heard of it."

"Let's try," she said.

"A village called Tora e Piccilli."

"They sent Jews there, didn't they?"

"How do you know?" I asked. I felt a shiver down my spine.

"Word gets around."

"Do you know any of them?"

"No, but I heard you helped them, that when the Germans

came, the documents with all their names went missing. You did what was right."

"We're only a small village," I said.

It seemed incredible that someone had heard what happened, and I was proud to hear her words.

"And Ferdinando? Did he know any of those who had been sent to us?"

"As much as me, I think." And then, in answer to a question I hadn't asked, she added: "That's how he is, always on the attack. He does it with everyone. It's his way of being. We have to accept ourselves for what we are."

Ferdinando joined us soon after. He'd been talking quietly to a man in a corner of the room.

"Davide, we're all amazed," Ferdinando said. "You still have much to do, but there are some interesting ideas. What you say is true. I didn't know you wrote."

"I work in the vinegar factory. I've never written."

"That's why there's always that smell around you." They all laughed. "I'm joking. There's nothing wrong with you. There's something deeply persuasive in your voice. I believed everything you said."

"Pigs," I said.

"What?"

"I spent my whole life looking after pigs in my father's pigsty. Pigs have no sense of humor. When I talked to them, I used basic words. I think it comes from that."

They looked at each other but said no more.

e walked, and meanwhile Ferdinando talked.

"You have to figure for yourself whether people like you: In the place we're going to, no one can applaud."

"What place is it?" I asked.

"An apartment block for those with money. Judges, lawyers, rich shit, people who would happily send the likes of us to prison, but in their own homes they treat us like exotic, amusing animals to show off to their friends. Each of us will be in a room, then we'll swap around."

"Whose house is it?"

"An architect who's rebuilding half of Naples. He'd just like to be young like we are, and so he invites us."

"And so he envies us," Claudia added.

"For the moment we take whatever spaces they give us."

"It's part of the Dictionary Project," Ferdinando continued. "Eventually we'll find theaters that are larger."

The main entrance door was open. It needed just a push. The stairs were like those in every building in that part of the city. Gray stone steps, white plaster, marble along the walls. We arrived at the apartment door, knocked, and one of the men we had seen at the rehearsal room came to open it. I was excited and scared at the same time. The house was full of people, and there were tables with bottles of wines and spirits, trays of sandwiches, and small rolls stuffed with prosciutto. I could eat whatever I wanted for free. Claudia saw me with my mouth full. I felt guilty, but she gave me a complicitous wink and opened her leather bag to show me what she was taking away. Then Eugenia, another girl from the company, arrived. "This will give me food for three days," she said, showing us a small candy bowl she had stolen at the entrance. "It should be worth a few lire."

Ferdinando came to tell us it was time to start.

I stood at the center, where the crowd had left a space. I looked into the eyes of the audience. They were exactly as Ferdinando had described them: respectably dressed, older than us. I did what I used to do in the pigsty when I stared at the animals to let them know I wasn't afraid.

I began my piece. Ferdinando and Claudia had told me not to go too fast, to think about nothing but the rhythm, the words, the voice, not to lose my concentration and, above all, that the words had to be clear. There was no other way of recounting pain than by describing the detail of everything that happened.

The people moved closer, taking up the few inches between us. I thought it was a good sign. I remembered what I'd been told: "Speak slowly, articulate every word, move your arms, look them in the eye, but focus also at a point on the wall, take a step toward the audience. Talk with the ghosts. Ask some question. Pretend to listen to an answer."

That was what I should have done that day when I dived into the stream. I should have been the first to jump.

Applause was not permitted. You had to know how it had

gone from the invisible energy that had been created. By the time I finished, the others had finished too. We changed rooms, then something unbelievable happened. Some people in the first room followed me into the second, so I found myself with the largest audience. I was intoxicated. My whole body was intoxicated.

People were following me at each change of room, and when I reached the last room, they were all around me. The other actors were leaning against a wall, waiting for me to finish. The whole audience was for me.

I had almost finished my last performance when I caught sight of a boy hurrying toward the door. I thought of Nicolas. It couldn't be. And so I faltered over the last words and lost my concentration. I had done the worst possible thing you can do on stage: I had started to think. I needed to be instinctive, I needed to continue living that real and invented life that I had begun in order to make the audience laugh—in the same way that everyone laughed when I imitated the cripple, which I did so well.

Ferdinando greeted me later with light applause.

"You were brilliant."

But his hand movements said something else. Rule number one: If you act, don't believe what other actors tell you.

"You are all they are talking about in this house," Claudia said.

Rule number two: Performing on stage attracts the women. This also has something to do with fear, and with its opposite, courage.

"But now we have to go. It's getting late," Ferdinando said. "Soon they'll all be leaving."

"Shall we go somewhere?" I was too excited to go to sleep.

"Everyone to their own home."

His tone had suddenly changed. The evening ended there. I took one last look at the people around me, hoping to catch one more glimpse of Nicolas's ghost.

During the night, the accumulated excitement drained away, and I felt exposed. It was foolish of me to get carried away over a performance that was no more than entertainment. I wrote until two o'clock, noting down things I shouldn't forget: not to lose my concentration, laughing and crying are the same thing, not to look too much at the audience, not to listen to noises in the room, not to follow the movements of those in front of you, once again not to lose concentration, make even longer pauses, each pause must last until it is broken by the audience, whisper, and lastly and most importantly, not to lose concentration. It's you who is driving the train; if you stop, then everyone stops.

I made notes around the margin: look for a less noisy room, eat more, smoke like every fashionable person I know, stop being scared, write a list of the girls I like.

When tiredness swept away every scrap of energy, I went to lie down, and once on the bed, everything was clear. I had used his words. I had moved like him. His arms, his hands had become mine. I had memorized everything Nicolas had said, every gesture, every position. Onstage I could be him.

IT WAS CLAUDIA WHO TOLD ME ABOUT THE PERFORmance in the cave at Posillipo.

"It's a mountain of yellow tufa with caves inside. The light doesn't reach inside, and it's very cold. Do you have a heavy jersey? I can bring you one, then you can let me have it back."

"Will we still be apart?"

"Ferdinando says we're not ready to work together. For the

moment it's better we each focus on our own character. If there are points of connection, they'll emerge by themselves."

"I don't have a character," I said.

"You do. It's a kind of double personality. The character doesn't absolve you, doesn't judge you. He's the outsider you bring into the womb when you are born and who speaks each time your main voice becomes distracted."

"It seems like a monster with two heads."

The road to the cave was uphill. I had brought an old brown shoulder bag I'd found in the storeroom at the vinegar factory. I had taken it to imitate Ferdinando, Claudia, Eugenia, and the others. Claudia was ahead, walking faster than me.

"Are you okay?" she asked.

"Go ahead. I don't want to slow you down."

"Shall I wait?"

"No. I can rehearse my part in the meantime."

There were many people in the caves. Ferdinando and Pietro, the other actor who helped organize the group, were already there. We would begin unannounced—our arrival was already part of the performance. I liked Ferdinando's ideas about new theater, even if his experimentation sometimes put the text in second place. For him, words were not everything.

I remained fascinated by the clandestine nature of the performances. Ferdinando would go alone to check out the spaces. "I've found somewhere," he would tell us during rehearsals when his search had been successful. So we knew something was about to happen.

It was then that I heard someone talking about me.

"Here's the cripple. Look, he's already performing. I heard him at the Rettifilo. He's the best."

A projection of me had already begun to exist outside my body.

In the silence that had been created, I let everyone hear my leg dragging on the ground, as I had done to provoke my father when we walked to Mass on Sundays. I exaggerated the movement just to annoy him. I'd been unconsciously rehearsing it for years. I could feel my heart pounding, and I wasn't sure the words would come to my aid as they had done the previous time. I opened the bag and pulled out two cardboard pigs I had made at home.

"Citizens of the caves, the time has come to create a new world."

I bent over one of the pigs, pretending it was whispering something in my ear.

"What did you say? After lunch, though? Good. Citizens, the new world will begin at exactly one p.m.!"

The laughter that greeted my arrival echoed around the cave. The same magic happened again. I had made a mental note of what I needed to do—speak more quickly at this point; change that word for something more exact, more detailed; get closer to the story being told.

At the end, Ferdinando made some closing remarks and gave general thanks. Intentionally, I kept one step behind as he added a few appropriate words.

"Let's go now," he said.

For that performance we received money. We went to a trattoria in Via dei Tribunali where they served wine and pasta with potatoes, which we ate noisily. I would have preferred to hurry back home to improve my monologue, and the dinner seemed a pointless waste of time. Even spending money like that was a luxury I could barely afford.

Pietro and Ferdinando kept their heads down over their bowls of pasta.

"We must find other performance spaces," I said. "Look for another audience."

Pietro was the first to speak: "You performed something different from what we had arranged."

He took another mouthful.

"You're doing so because you want to stand above the others. This isn't what our work is about."

"That doesn't seem so bad," I said. "We can improve the arrangement. Maybe we need to question what idea we have."

Ferdinando stopped chewing what was in his mouth. "Davide's ambitions are different from ours," he said. "No one can tell him what to do or not to do. We're an open group, and we will remain open. If everyone moved toward Davide, there's only one explanation. He's the best. As Pietro said, our purpose is different. We're not interested in individuality. We have other rules. We have to accept the fact that Davide is more talented, and this is no longer the place for him."

I stood up, unsteady on my feet. This company was all I had, but I knew they were right. My need to act had more to do with revenge than with theater. Claudia stood up, gave me a big hug, and said: "Good luck, Davide. The cardboard pigs are fantastic."

I left, feeling a crushing pain in my bones. I went back along the same street and turned out of Via dei Tribunali not knowing how I would ever find another audience. That day, I had wanted more but had suddenly lost everything.

"Davide," I heard someone call.

He was a man of around fifty, balding, well-dressed.

"That's your name, right? I'm Paolo Marino. I saw you at the caves. I was really struck by your performance."

"That's very kind," I said.

"I'd like to ask you something. You're not pretending to drag your leg, right? I saw you walking just now. I had already noticed during your act. It hadn't occurred to anyone in the audience, but you might say it's one of the rules of theater, no?"

He looked down at my leg. He touched the outer part.

"I'm an orthopedic surgeon. Does it hurt if I touch here?"

"No."

"Can I ask you to walk forward and then back, holding your arms down by your sides?"

I did as he asked.

"Like this?"

"Yes."

I moved ten steps away, then came back toward him.

"Maybe I could help you," he said.

"What do you mean?"

"I mean your leg. You'll never be a great runner, that's clear, but maybe a good walker."

"Are you serious?"

"I listened to your monologue at the caves, and I know how our body affects our lives, especially when it's limiting. I think you spoke more truth than the audience realized."

 went to visit him at the hospital just a month later. He approached as soon as he saw me sitting on the bench in the ward corridor.

"I was thinking you wouldn't come," he said. "I have another patient now. I'll call you when I've finished."

The few doctors we had seen in the village dealt only with fevers or measles. Not even Furtunà had ever been treated for what he called his "weakness of the lungs." He had been born that way, and no one could do anything about it. We knew about pig diseases and plant parasites. We knew when an animal was about to die, when it might infect others, or when there were nut weevils digging away inside the chestnut trees. But we, as humans, knew nothing about ourselves and could only pray for someone to save us—Jesus Christ, for example, or the Madonna of Pompei, or Mussolini.

I said nothing at the vinegar factory until the last day, so the owner was angry. I should have told him earlier and now, because of me, he'd be one person short. "But you've done the right thing," he said at last. "You're young. You have your whole life ahead." Whatever the outcome of the operation, we both knew that my job at the vinegar factory was over.

ALONG THE HOSPITAL WALLS THERE WERE WHITE TILES and metal lockers.

"Has no one come to be with you when you leave the operating theater?" Dr. Marino asked.

"I have no one," I said.

"Not even your friends at the theater?"

"They've decided they're no longer my friends."

"It'll be some time before you can walk again."

"I know."

"You're still sure you want to go through with it?"

"Yes."

"It's normal to be afraid."

"I can't turn back."

"I understand. Now breath in and count to twenty."

I have a few memories of the large lamp above me. I watched the metal as it twisted and turned to liquid, then the walls of the room as they bent. I was awake, no longer in control. My last thought went to Teresa.

When I reopened my eyes, a yellowish light filtered into the room. I didn't know what time it was, or whether it was the sun or the lamp.

"Don't worry, it's the anesthetic. It makes you feel tired."

I saw my mother sitting beside my bed, but the vision quickly faded. On the chair there was just the bag I had brought with me.

"Davide?"

The voice came from far away, then suddenly seemed beside

me or inside my brain. My body then felt shock waves. The intermittence of contact.

"Does it hurt if I touch you here?"

I felt nothing.

"It's the anesthetic. Don't worry."

I was in the grip of a deep sleep.

Notes for a monologue: A man discovers he no longer has a body. He's dead but doesn't yet know it. He feels light and invincible, but he realizes that someone who can't feel pain can't feel pleasure. Conclusion: Pain and happiness are the same thing.

"I'll be back in a while. I've asked a nurse to come and check on you each hour. Once we're sure it has gone well, we can start the therapy, and in the meantime, you'll eat the worst broth of your life."

I spent the whole night immobile without knowing what was in store. I had a stomachache but couldn't get up. Over the next few days, the nurses helped me out of bed. I had to walk with a stick as far as a certain point in the room. I was still moving in my usual way.

"It's instinct, habit. That will change."

I tried putting one foot behind the other. I wasn't swaying. My back didn't shift about. My movement was straight.

I REMAINED IN MY ROOM FOR SEVERAL WEEKS DURING which I did the exercises they had shown me in the hospital. I behaved like the obedient patient who did what he was told. I wondered what I would do if the operation hadn't had the desired effect. There were frequent visits to the outpatient clinic, and the doctor's questions were always the same. Did my back hurt? Did I feel stronger on the other leg? Over that period, I wrote a short monologue called "The Convalescent."

When I recovered, Cuncè organized a small lunch for me. The smell of ragù came up from the kitchen. It had been cooking since the morning, and a girl who worked part-time for her brought me fried anchovies and cake. When I told her I would soon be vacating the room, Cuncè said she had seen me arrive as a boy and I would be leaving as a man, and it was right after all to look for somewhere less damp than that room. I thanked her for the lunch, and she hugged me and gave me the leftover anchovies.

Later on, as the weeks passed, when I was walking straight and even my shadow looked better, I thought I should tell the story about Ferdinando and Claudia, about Cuncè, about the jobs I had done, about the operation, and about my life, which was gradually changing as the days passed. I should talk about the distance that had been created between what I was and what I had become, and about me, and how I continued to keep myself separate from everything.

I FOUND A JOB AT THE MOLLICA CERAMICS FACTORY. THE notice said: "Nonskilled jobs also available." When the personnel manager arrived, he told us we would be starting that very day, no questions asked. He had sheets of paper on which we had to write our names. He took us to a man at a desk saying, "Here are the new ones."

I moved to a house closer to the factory in an area I'd never been to. They called it "the brides block" because several newlyweds had moved there over the past year. It wasn't romantic in any way. It was the poorest building in the district, so poor that hard-up couples could find a single room with an inside bathroom for just a few lire.

In the factory I worked at the kiln. I repeated identical movements, and meanwhile I kept myself apart, adding phrases to my monologue. I was fascinated by the machines and more at ease working at the production line for ordinary objects like plates than in the craft department where skilled workers created small statues of doves or sailing ships. I thought about the pigs for the show, how they needed to be larger, made of cloth, like large pink toys.

After working for a few minutes, my body moved by itself. A product had to be fed into the machines at one end, and it came out at the other. I thought of applying certain factory processes to the pieces I was writing. I felt the influence of the machines, and several sketches grew out of this fascination, such as the one about the man engaged to be married to a mechanical press and the accusation that he was being placed under continual pressure. The joke was crude and simple, but it worked. Ferdinando was right when he said that the new would sweep us away.

I heard that several workers were secretly meeting and printing leaflets that were being passed around in the canteen. They were encouraging workers to join the union to fight for better working conditions. The idea of the man engaged to marry the mechanical press had come to me while reading those leaflets. I found one of them in the canteen that said: "Did you know you spend more time at the press than with your wife?" I realized those words already contained stories.

I got to know a girl in the paint shop. A friend of hers came to tell me she fancied me but that she hadn't the courage to say so. She pointed her out among the other girls. When I went to chat to her in the canteen, she tidied the blond hair under her green cap. I was no longer limping. I groomed my hair and spoke Italian that was good, certainly better than what I heard among the other workers in the paint shop or at the kiln. The girl told me we could go into the paint storeroom to talk alone.

It was the first time I made love in Naples without paying for it.

I was about to ask if we could see each other outside the factory when she told me there was a boy on her street who wanted to marry her. We stopped meeting in the storeroom, and after a while she stopped smiling at me. Soon we forgot all about each other.

At Christmas there was a small entertainment to which workers could take their families. Some offered to sing, others would read poems. I went to the head of the department and asked if I could perform my monologue. They kept me waiting two weeks for the answer, then one day he called me and said the answer was yes.

There was a real stage and a curtain that would open when I asked. I stitched the pigs by hand and made the costume. I knew my script well, and if I forgot any words I could improvise. I was clear about the direction I was going in.

I pulled the cloth pigs out of my bag, arranged them as I had rehearsed at home, and everyone began laughing. I pretended to forget how to organize them. I first put the little ones in front, then the big one, then measured them with my hands. I took a step toward the audience, pretending this time to limp, and began the opening line.

I didn't know there was a journalist in the audience, invited by the workers who had written the leaflets, or that my face would appear the next day in the city's biggest newspaper. I didn't know that six months later I would leave the factory to become a professional actor.

or years I would go each morning to study at the Royal Palace library. I came to know the world through dusty books that had a number on their spine and lay on their designated shelf. It was not the real world but its reconstruction through words.

The Davide who had left Tora was disappearing, being replaced by another who bought new clothes, started going to parties, and played a part in the life of a country that saw a bright future before it after the hardships of the war.

My body had changed: It had become that of a man. I was lean, slender. I went to a barber in Piazza del Plebiscito who groomed my beard and tended my hair. I told myself that it was for work, but it was vanity.

I went with women, in and out of brothels, but could never manage a stable relationship. A piece of me was missing, and that missing part formed the basis for my work in the theater. That emptiness was my driving force.

On some mornings I would walk along the avenues of the new zoological park in Naples. Elephants, giraffes, bright-colored parrots, lions, tigers—I was fascinated by those majestic animals, so different from those I knew when I lived in the countryside. There were few visitors during the week, apart from me, and I spent the mornings studying the idiosyncrasies the animals had developed from being fenced up every day. In some cases, they were the same as the factory assembly line or departments where the pace of work was frenetic. The zoo had recently opened and was part of the modernity that had suddenly and aggressively arrived.

It was impossible not to be seduced by the carefree atmosphere of that period: an atmosphere I had never known, almost a collective inebriation. Fashions had changed, and music too. Objects of little importance were now essential.

I heard the first edition of the Sanremo Music Festival on the radio at a girlfriend's house at the end of January 1951. We joked about the simplicity of those tunes, and their childish words, but in the streets the next day we heard people singing the winning entry.

Then, when television appeared, people gathered around to watch the programs. I wondered what would happen to the theaters and how long my performances would survive when people could now watch a show every night in their own homes. Time had passed me by, and I seemed to have been trapped somewhere. Twelve years had passed since my arrival in Naples, and nothing was the same.

When I was asked what my monologues were about, I'd say, "About the passage of time. It's the only thing I can write about."

The first real theater in which I performed was not far from the place where I had rehearsed with Ferdinando and Claudia, which in the meantime had become first a carpenter's workshop and then a produce store.

There were music shows every evening. A woman sang classic Neapolitan songs and American hits, accompanied on the piano.

Giuseppina Acampora changed her name to Josephine Porà, Antonietta Maddaluno became Antonya Bellaluna. When they asked me to change my name, I said no. Once the singers had gone, few spectators were left in the hall. Almost all of them had nowhere else to go. Those down-and-outs had been my first audience, an army of discontents looking for someone who spoke the truth.

I did two shows a night, seven days a week. The first was more crowded, and I performed pieces by Eduardo Scarpetta and Eduardo De Filippo. Ferdinando would have accused me of selling out, but it was part of the contract, and with them I learned how to make an audience laugh. It was my job, my craft, to become familiar with the bodies of those strangers sitting in front of me, and with my own body. When I wore the mask of Pulcinella, I became aggressive, petulant. I felt protected by the hood. In the second show, where there was a more desperate audience, I performed with no mask.

I was paid less than I had earned at the Mollica ceramics factory at Capodimonte. The theater owner sometimes sent a dish of spaghetti to my dressing room or gave me clothes he no longer wanted.

Only over time did I finally pull down Pulcinella's mask, when the number of spectators in the second performance reached and was eventually larger than the first. For a while I called the show *Unmasked*.

The theater owner raised the ticket price without a drop in audience. I no longer had to work every day, and during those unexpected moments of freedom I could walk around the city and visit new bars that had opened in the city center.

I was alone in the theater, in the darkness and the silence of my dressing room. I walked along the corridor and out of the rear door. Via Toledo was now deserted. I walked to a restaurant in the Spanish quarter. The bell above the door drew the attention of everyone at the tables. Emma approached when she saw me.

"It's late," she said. "Not your usual time."

"I was held up in the dressing room. I think the doorman was waiting for me to leave so he could close the theater."

"Another one who hates you. You look tired." Emma lifted her arm and stroked back a wisp of hair from my forehead. A swift, maternal gesture.

"How did it go?" she asked, then continued without waiting for an answer. "I'll decide for you. Pork cutlets with lemon." She sat for a moment on the seat beside me. "Your face is just as white, with or without greasepaint."

"I'm tired, that's all. I sleep little."

"You've said that for as long as I've known you."

I looked around at the people in the restaurant. I usually noted their mannerisms. A man who cut his meat into tiny pieces and arranged them symmetrically around the plate. A well-dressed middle-aged couple who didn't talk. Everything became part of my sketch. Emma came back a few minutes later.

"Davide, there's a person looking for you, a woman. She's at the entrance."

"Do you know her?" I asked.

"She said her name is Immacolata."

I looked at the entrance where the woman was waiting.

"Tell her to come."

I watched Immacolata make her way between the tables, choosing the longer route to gain time, a sign that it wasn't easy for her either. I kept so few memories that I could make no comparison between the girl at the engagement party and the woman who was now moving slowly in my direction. She looked thinner, her skin perhaps better cared for. Generally more attractive, I would have said. Some bodies reach their full beauty only after adolescence. I guessed that our failed relationship had also brought some kind of benefit.

She was there in front of me. I stood and gave a slight bow, a gesture that I did very well.

"Immacolata," I said.

"Don't get up."

"Please sit down."

"May I?"

"But of course. I'm alone. Will you eat something?"

"I've eaten, thank you."

I didn't know what to say.

"I saw you and came in," she said.

"You did right."

"That's not true. I followed you here, then came in. I saw your photograph on the theater billboard. I wanted to go in, but the ticket was too expensive. I waited outside, then followed you."

"Are you all right for money? Do you need anything?"

"No, I don't need anything," she replied.

"Excuse me, I didn't want to pry. Are you still at Tora?"

She looked at me for a moment. "My husband is the foreman of a shoe factory. We live just outside Naples. We're here because his parents aren't well. Old age is a horrible business."

"I hope it's nothing serious."

She moved toward me, almost as if to prompt me, lowering her voice imperceptibly. "You can stop acting now. This is no theater, so far as I know."

"I'm sorry, but I don't know what to say."

"Then don't say anything."

"So tell me why you've come to sit here."

She was no longer the girl who had been embarrassed at showing me what would be the children's room.

"I work too, you know. The canning industry. *'E pummarole*," she added in dialect. Tomatoes. "I get backaches and sometimes fall asleep in the minibus that takes us from the station to the factory. All the same, I've been much worse than this. Like when I thought you'd gone off because of me."

"I'm sorry for what I did. It wasn't your fault, Immacolata. I was young. Today it would have been different."

"You ran off when the Jewish boy vanished. I thought at first it was because you didn't want me. I was too young as well. I couldn't understand. But it was for him."

I wondered how long she'd been preparing that speech and how many times she'd rehearsed it.

"I wanted to get away too, but I didn't have the strength. I had to marry to do so." Her voice was passionate but firm. She knew exactly what to say. "We searched for you in the woods. I thought we'd find you dead. I hoped we would. I hoped to see you hanging from a branch or with your head in the stream. Many thought you had taken advantage of me and then run off."

"I'm sorry to have made you suffer so much."

"We come from the same place, even though you now play the gentleman. Your mother went almost mad with pain, then she too decided you were dead, that they had buried you in the fields. But after a few months the other one vanished too."

"Who?"

"The girl, Teresa."

"She vanished?" I asked, with almost a shriek.

"I know she's living in Naples now. Has a husband, children, works as a nurse."

She suddenly stood up.

"What do you know about my family?" I asked.

She studied me closely. "But have you really never gone back?"

I made no reply.

"It's not normal for someone to go off and vanish forever. My father once told me they're no longer living there. But I don't know where." She looked once again at my clothes. "I have to go now. When we were living in the village, we got it all wrong, but I don't know if it's any better now."

She took a few steps toward the exit, then turned toward me.

"Just one last thing."

"What's that?"

"I saw you as you walked here. How come you don't limp anymore?"

long the corridors of the orthopedic ward there were white radiators. The heat had worn away the paint, and the natural cast-iron color could be seen around the edges. I arrived with no appointment, as I had always done. We hadn't seen each other for some time. Dr. Marino sometimes waited for me outside the theater, at the stage door, and we would go to a small bar with tables looking onto the street. He would have a liqueur. I'd have a tonic water. He would ask the waiters a load of questions about liqueurs and in the end would order two "for comparison."

He was more and more busy after that, and I changed too. I went about only with theater people: I performed on and off stage. I felt devoured by something inside me. It was a moment in my life when I lacked nothing, yet I still felt as lost as I had been on the first day.

I waited in the corridor for the appointments to end, and when the consulting room door opened, I made sure the doctor could see me.

"My dear Davide, consultations have finished, but I can always make time for a theater star."

"It's not for a consultation this time," I said.

"Come, it's a pleasure to see you," he said, giving me a hug. "You're looking great. Anyway, I'm not the one who says you're a star. It's the newspapers."

"I was in the area and wanted to say hello."

I took a few steps toward him. I already knew which part of my pelvis he would be looking at, then how he would follow the movement of my feet. I tried not to adopt an awkward posture or distort the way I walked.

I sat on one of the chairs in front of his desk.

"If I hadn't met you, my life would have been different."

"You overestimate me. I prescribe foot supports and tell children how to sit with their backs straight," he said with a smile.

"I'm here to ask a favor."

I needed to get straight to the point.

"From your tone of voice, it seems like something important. Let's see if I can help."

"Is there a register with the names of every nurse?"

"In this hospital?"

"In every hospital in Naples."

He gave a deep sigh.

"Well that's a difficult question."

"As you say, it is. I'll give you the name of the person I'm looking for, and perhaps you'd know who to ask. Maybe it's just a matter of time."

"Do you know at least what unit she works in? That would help."

"All I know is she's a nurse."

"We're looking for a needle in a haystack, but I'll do my best."

I wrote "Teresa Glicine" on a piece of paper.

It was the first time I had written down her full name. It was amazing that I had never done so before, at Tora, when I was closed inside the pigsty searching for words on which I could practice. I slid the paper over the table, he read it, paused over it longer than necessary, perhaps to reread it, then folded it up.

"Is it urgent?" he asked.

"I've waited a long time. I don't suppose there's any hurry at this point."

"It rather seems the opposite."

That evening I met a journalist, Irene, who had interviewed me the previous week. She had already written articles about my work. It was easy to find her in bars in the city center or around Piazza del Plebiscito. "The night owl"—that's what I called her. She was restless too. You could feel a sort of vibration when you stood near to her. She was always on the move, never happy wherever she was. The night spots were where she searched out the material for her articles. She told me about a piece she was working on, and as she spoke, she shook her wrist full of metal and ivory bracelets.

"I remember your first performances in that empty theater. You were good, but I thought you'd flop, as they all flop."

"Thanks for the confidence," I said.

We were at an outside table.

"I've seen plenty of them disappear, but you're still around. I've often thought about you. What a shame you're so young," she laughed. "My God, I must have drunk too much."

She moved her hand in the air as if she were wiping something from the blackboard. "Forget everything," she said.

The Neapolitan sky could sometimes take on a blueness that cannot be described, like the pinkness of sunsets. I still found the city somber and dark, contrary to the way its inhabitants described it.

At a certain point, somebody called her. She tended to smile whenever she heard her name.

"What will you do after this show?" she asked.

"I haven't yet decided," I said. "But I think I'll stay awhile longer. It's the only thing I know."

"You always have a look of sadness, an old-fashioned sadness."

"Didn't you know, a touch of sadness helps to keep you young? Young people are always rather sad."

"I'm the saddest and loneliest woman in the universe. I'm falling to pieces. Look at my face," she said with a laugh. "But no more drink, otherwise I won't manage to get home this evening."

In the meantime, a woman came up to her. She was wearing a light blue dress, large, perhaps intentionally one size bigger, maybe a new London fashion.

"Come," Irene said. "Sit with us."

"I can't stay long. Tomorrow morning, my alarm clock goes off early."

"How boring you are, you who live by day. Stop for just a minute. This is Davide," she said, pointing at me.

"I know who he is," the woman replied, holding her hand in my direction. "I'm Agnese. I have to be in Rome for the newspaper tomorrow morning, and then in the evening there's the launch of a new theater company. In fact, that's what it calls itself: the Company."

"Is that all?" Irene asked.

"Yes. It's causing quite a stir in Rome. Their shows are disorderly, unscripted, and announced just a few days before. So I'm leaving at the last minute."

"Why all the mystery?" I asked.

"It's said all the actors are Jewish, that all were deported."

I swallowed involuntarily.

"Group therapy?" Irene asked.

"Could be," said Agnese, who in the meantime was chewing an olive she had taken from our table. "It's said that some stay silent throughout, and others talk about their life beforehand. And that's the most powerful part, because beforehand we were all the same."

"Are they all from Rome?" I asked.

"I don't know. They have a number tattooed on their arm, and they call themselves by that."

"They've given up their names?"

"They've written a manifesto. They say they had no name apart from the number tattooed on their arm. They talk about their life beforehand like a dream, something that had never really happened."

Agnese was gesticulating, looking around her, eating the olives. I felt suddenly alive and afraid, overwhelmed by memories.

he train for Rome left twenty minutes late, with no explanation.

I was in no hurry to get there. I seemed to be the only one who wasn't. When the train moved off, I wondered why I still thought Nicolas was alive after all those years. Maybe he'd been shot, maybe he'd managed to escape and no longer wished to see me. Yet even if our destinies seemed forever divided, I could never stop searching for him.

There was a woman in the seat opposite.

"Do you mind if I open the window?" she asked.

I pulled the window down and the wind ruffled her hair. She wore a long gray skirt. Her ankles appeared when she crossed her legs. I studied the lines of her face while she concentrated on reading a magazine. Her straight nose, the severe line of her bangs, and her green trench coat told me she was a woman who would never talk to strangers. Since my discovery that Teresa might not be far away, my recollection of her body had emerged from deep in my memory as if it had always been fixed there.

The train pulled into Formia station. It wasn't a scheduled stop.

One of the station staff walked past our carriage.

"Will we be here long?" asked a passenger sitting nearby.

"We're waiting for them to tell us to move on. There's been an accident ahead, a vehicle on the tracks."

The man took a pack of cigarettes from his suitcase and lit one. He took short, continual puffs without ever removing it from his lips. There was an intermittent flicker of burning ash. I studied the movement and imitated it. I brought an imaginary cigarette to my mouth and thought it would be an interesting movement to include in the monologue. I'd have to work hard at conveying the sensation of filling my mouth with smoke, but a question like "What time does this train leave?" also seemed a good start for something.

At Termini station in Rome, I took a taxi to the theater where the Company would be meeting to rehearse. I'd been to Rome more than once over the years, enjoying less success there than in Naples. "Naples is a world of its own," said the owner of the first theater in which I worked. After the show I always went to dine with somebody. I would spend the night listening to what was going on in Rome theaters and realized there were always new influences in Rome. I could see Naples more clearly whenever I moved away from it.

"We're here," said the taxi driver, who had driven the whole time without saying a word. The theater was still closed.

"Where can I eat around here?" I asked.

"There aren't any restaurants, but you'll find some bars that sell sandwiches. There's one further down this street."

The bar the taxi driver had pointed to was closer than I realized. From it I could keep an eye on the theater entrance. While I was pondering the unappetizing roll with prosciutto that the young waitress had brought me on a plate, I saw a woman open the side door. Other people arrived over the next few minutes. I sat watching them, then paid and set off, feeling a quiver in my legs.

The theater was small, and its upper windows were covered with black cloth to stop the light entering from the street. I sat in one of the back rows. There were six people onstage, four men and two women. I was sure that none of the men was Nicolas, however much he might have changed. They had arranged themselves symmetrically, an arm's length apart, in two rows. It was a simple, predictable layout, but it had a powerful visual effect. The six, in that grid-like arrangement, became a single body.

While their monologues followed one after another, I felt the darkness loom over the theater and envelop everything: the traffic, the buildings in the area, the railway tracks, which couldn't have been far away. And I, as the sole spectator, had to sustain the whole dramatic impact. Having heard them, nothing could be spared. All the stories merged into a single story that made my arms shake. I had no idea whether they knew of my presence.

Only their long silence persuaded me that the rehearsal was over. They put on their coats and headed toward the exit without stopping to talk. I decided to approach the woman I had first seen, the one who had opened the theater. She looked so ordinary that she made me think her role might have been marginal and her story different and less traumatic. She had thin arms and, on closer observation, was older than I had imagined. Her girlish body had deceived me.

"Good afternoon," I said.

It was only then that she seemed to notice me. She was sitting behind a small desk at the entrance, the one from which the tickets would be sold, and was sorting some papers.

"Hello," she said.

"I listened to your rehearsal. Maybe I shouldn't. I came in without permission."

"Anyone can enter," she said, without looking up. "You've done nothing wrong. There are usually a few more. Did you like it?"

"I liked it but need time to make up my mind. I'm a slow audience."

"That's already something. I think it might be regarded as a positive response."

"I think it might."

"It's not an easy play, and perhaps it's not a play at all. You will have understood this for yourself."

I seemed to have told her exactly what she wanted to hear.

"But you've come for another reason," she continued.

"Yes," I said, feeling that I'd been unmasked.

"It's the same for everyone who comes to see us. What do you want to know? Whether it's all true? Is that what interests you?"

There was a moment of silence.

"I'm looking for someone," I said.

This was the second time in just a few days that I had used these words.

"An actor?"

"I don't even know if he went where you went. It's possible. This is just an attempt on my part."

"We don't ask a lot of questions here. Our group is open. These people come to talk about themselves for reasons that are sometimes not apparent to others, sometimes not even to themselves."

I told her about Nicolas, about his father, and what I knew about their family.

"But I cannot help you," the woman said. "Nobody here knows anyone's name. We call each other by our last three numbers."

She lifted the sleeve of her blouse and showed me the tattoo on her forearm.

"I'm 149. That's how the others know me."

I wasn't sure what to say.

"But if you are here, it must be very important," she said.

"I'm looking for this person because I cannot stop looking for him."

"Then I hope you'll be able to tell him yourself."

I held my hand out to shake hers, not sure whether she would respond. After a momentary hesitation she placed her bony hand in mine. I apologized that I couldn't stay for the evening performance and told her about my work in the theater.

I left Rome that same afternoon on the first train. On the way back, I persuaded myself that Nicolas was dead and that the journey to Rome had been a way of coming to terms with his loss. The journey, the performance, the return on foot to the station, everything seemed to be a metaphor for a funeral celebrated too late. Perhaps it wasn't true that I was looking for him. Perhaps I just wanted to talk to someone about him, to say that I had known him, that I was wounded by his absence, that I would never get over it.

I felt a liberation when the train arrived at Naples station.

Over the following weeks I finished writing my new monologue, though I didn't know what would happen to me after what I thought would be my last show.

 spent the evening at a bar in Via Partenope with Irene and her intellectual friends from Milan. There was a young woman, Sofia, with whom I spent the whole evening talking. She was a sensuous woman, with a dress cut low at the back. She had lived in Spain for a long while, was interested in current trends in European art, and wanted to write about them.

"My friend has eyes only for you, Davide," Irene said. Sofia blushed. But I was tired and restless. I hated discussions about art or theater that had political messages. I preferred the messages written by the workers at the ceramics factory in their leaflets: "Fuck the bosses," "Sabotage the machines," "Let's stop production." After working ten hours consecutively at the kiln or in the paint shop, they didn't have the energy to write too many words, so they kept it short.

I could see that Sofia was disappointed when I said I was going.

"Stay a little longer, Davide," Irene said. "You don't have to go right now?"

I just wanted to walk.

When I got home, I found Dr. Marino kneeling and sliding something under my door.

"There you are. I'm too old to be slipping notes under doors, though as a young man I did it more than once. You won't believe it, but I used to write some terrible poems and foisted them on girls I'd fallen in love with. It was often their fathers or brothers who discovered them first, and I had to keep out of the way for a while."

I gave him a hand to get up.

"I thought you'd be at home," he said.

"Come on in."

"I didn't want to bother you."

"It's no bother. I have a liqueur. I'm sure you'll like it. As you know, I don't drink alcohol and can't tell you whether it's as good as they say. It was a gift from some people who came to the show."

"I shouldn't say it, but I also have patients who give me bottles of wine or things they've made themselves. I don't see why I should refuse such things."

We went inside, and he sat down on the only chair in the kitchen.

"I see you like receiving guests."

He looked around as if he were trying to figure out my relationship with the few items of furniture about. They'd been there since I moved in, and over the years I'd felt no need to buy anything new.

"You know, Davide, I've sometimes wondered what kind of life you lead. You've always been a source of mystery and of strength. I think I've even envied it."

"There's nothing to envy about me," I said.

"Don't get me wrong. I wouldn't swap my life for that of

anyone else. It's taken me years to become the person I wanted to be."

"So you think it takes strength to choose what to be?"

"I'd have to think about that one, but I think the answer has something to do with what's to come. And with fear."

"Fear of what?" I asked.

"For example, your fear now. In this note I have what you asked me, but you haven't the courage to take it." All this time he'd been holding the piece of paper with the information I wanted.

"This person must really frighten you," Dr. Marino said.

"Something that frightens us can only attract us," I said.

I poured some liqueur into the glass. The doctor took a sip, held it in his mouth, then clenched his jaw to absorb the strength of its taste.

"I agree with the person who gave it to you. It's truly excellent. I had good reason to come here after all."

"Take it. I won't be drinking it. I'd be happy if you took it with you."

"No, I'd end up drinking it all. You keep it. I'll have an excuse to come and see you."

The doctor then turned toward the door.

"So far as that information," he added, "I'd prefer you not say I had anything to do with it."

As soon as I was alone, I opened the note. I found Teresa's name in my writing, and below it, in the doctor's familiar hand, the hospital unit in which she worked.

I had walked past it so many times over the years without realizing we might have run into each other.

I tore the paper into four pieces, threw it in the garbage bin, then went to lie down. The windows were open, and I could hear music from a distant bar. I had heard it said that Naples is the southernmost district of New York, or the northernmost capital of Africa.

During the night I returned to the kitchen to retrieve the four bits of paper from the garbage bin. I stuck the pieces back together, then pinned them to a board.

It seemed that I had no choice, that I had never had one.

ver the years I had kept a constant picture of Teresa undressing in front of me and Nicolas, seen from every possible angle. I remembered the exact movement when she let her dress slip down, the first uncertain attempt to cover her bra with her hands, then her allowing Nicolas to see it, and finally her leap from the platform as an invitation to follow her. A splendid declaration of love: For you I give up the earth beneath my feet. That was the picture that I followed during my shows, without ever arriving at the great moment of her legs flailing in the air prior to the impact with the water. I repeated that leap hundreds of times in front of a distracted, sleepy, occasionally attentive audience, without ever truly transmitting the magnificence of her action, her courage. Without ever being sure that others would launch themselves behind me.

Teresa's leap made me dizzy. It was the truest image I have ever had of a woman.

IN FRONT OF THE HOSPITAL ENTRANCE WAS A GARDEN with a path and two symmetrical lines of dark, porous stone benches. The market stalls set up nearby mixed the crowd of hospital patients with those who were buying fly-ridden meat, fruit, vegetables, loose pasta, oil on tap, secondhand shoes. I thought Teresa would pass that way. The hospital had countless side entrances, but it still seemed more likely she would use the main door. Perhaps she was on her ward and I would have to pretend to meet her by chance, like a scene in the theater: A man wakes one morning with a strange lump on his chest and arrives at the hospital to find that the nurse who could assist him is the woman he is secretly in love with, and she tells him that to save him they'll have to perform an urgent operation to remove his heart.

I decided instead to remain on the bench, with other people around, holding a newspaper that I couldn't manage to read. After a whole morning spent like that, I left. Perhaps I didn't really want to meet her. I didn't bother for the next few days, but the work I was doing with words, my continual delving into memory, the relentless search for lines, compelled me to return to those realms of thought in which the waters are never calm.

So I went back to the hospital, still trying to imagine the woman she must have become after more than ten years. Yet when I saw her hurrying through the flow of people toward the main entrance, the first thing I did was superimpose my memory onto what I saw. Her fashionable coat gave me the impression of a woman anxious in some way about what other people thought.

I remained there on the bench, allowing her to pass, and at that moment I had the feeling she wouldn't want to meet me. It was more than a guess. My photo had appeared in the newspapers over the years, and my name was often on the playbill in the glass case by the theater entrance.

I studied her back and her neck, her leather bag, which was

worn around the corners, the tight mesh of her dark stockings. But then, as if I had called out to her, she stopped. She stood still. For how many seconds? Less than the time it had taken her to dive from the platform that day. It required less courage now. She turned and walked hesitantly toward me. She sat by me on the bench as if we'd been sitting there for over ten years without speaking.

"I finish at four. There's a bar at the rear exit. They have an upstairs room inside with tables. If you're not busy, we can meet there. It's difficult for me here."

"All right, we'll meet later where you said."

She got up and walked quickly to make up for the lost seconds.

I repeated to myself the instructions she had given me. We seemed like two spies.

I went to the bar where we would meet. I sat at a table by a large window in a green metal frame. I asked a waiter for some sheets of paper and a pen with the promise that I would pay him for them, then started to jot down a few notes, waiting until it was four o'clock. My starting point was the two lines of conversation we had just had. Around lunchtime I ate half a sandwich, watching the people who came and went.

Shortly after four, Teresa came up the stairs to the first floor and sat at my table. She put her bag on the empty seat and looked for a moment at the few lines I had written on the paper.

"There's only one doctor who can do that leg operation," she said.

"Do you know him?" I asked.

"He's a friend of my husband. Once, during a dinner at Ischia, I heard him talk about you. I didn't know it was you, but every detail that he added led me in your direction. It seemed incredible."

"It was he who suggested the operation. What did he say?"

"Do you want to know?"

"Why not?"

"Well, I suppose we never know anyone deep down."

"What did he say?"

She started fumbling in her pocket.

"He talked first about an actor who came from outside and did sketches based on his life as a pig keeper. He was amused by you, by your strange dialect and the bizarre stories you went around telling."

"I don't think that's so bad."

"He talked to me without realizing you and I spoke in the same way. I told no one I knew you."

"Why?"

"I don't know. It was hard to talk about. I sometimes think about you, but I'm not sure how, in what way. Perhaps I shouldn't say it." There was a pause. She fingered a bracelet. "I went to see you at the theater. I was with my husband. It was strange. At first, I couldn't understand the words because the excitement of seeing you muddled everything. What you said was real while everyone else thought it was made up."

She kept her eyes shut for a moment—she hadn't changed so much after all. Maybe her arms, yes, they were thinner, more nervous. Her hair was different too. It lay over her ears, altering the outline of the face I knew so well. It was a style I had seen in advertisements for hair products. Teresa called a waiter and ordered sparkling water. She said thank you twice. "How long can you stay?" I asked.

I said it in a moment of confusion, and Teresa didn't even answer.

"I don't know how you managed to find me. Perhaps Marino

told you about me, but there's no point discussing it." She paused. "Are you happy?" she asked.

I was caught by surprise.

"I've never thought about it."

She looked toward the exit. I could hear waiters talking in a side room. Teresa touched her lips with her left hand, squeezing them.

"You're wondering why I've never gone looking for you," she added.

"You didn't have to."

"But I did. You can't imagine how much." She breathed in sharply through her nose.

"I don't know if I'm happy," I said, replying too late to her question. She gave a faint smile, the first since she had arrived at the bar, and I felt her back release all its tension. I fooled myself for an instant that we might still in some way be the same and that all our futile words might evaporate as soon as one of us had embraced the other.

"When I left Tora, I told them I was going away to study. I found a place in a college run by nuns. There was silence, and I liked it. I trained to be a nurse and lived in a solitude so deep that I didn't know it could exist. When the war ended, I went to Rome and stayed there working for a while. It was only later that I came to Naples. I met Carlo at the hospital where I am now. He's older than me, a well-respected doctor. He has lived in Paris and Madrid. I told him about my situation, and we became much closer. His friends didn't accept me at first. They thought I was taking advantage, and maybe they weren't so wrong. A single woman with two young children and just looking for somewhere safe. The gossipmongers are always right in the end, aren't they? You could put that in one of your shows."

She lit a cigarette.

It was all wrong. The conversation wasn't moving in the direction I had imagined for so many years. I ought to have been asking about the straps of her swimming costume, whether the sun still left a mark that would take over a month to disappear. Whether she knew who read letters to the old people in the village, whether the workers in her father's rope factory remembered the time when she wanted to learn everything. Or I ought to have told her about when I went around the bars trying to fall in love with a woman who wasn't her.

"Why have we still not spoken about him?" I asked instead.

She shifted in her chair.

"You're always the same, Davide. This is what you came for, to talk about him." She rested a fingernail on her half-finished glass of water. "I was the one who threw the petrol bomb at the German truck. They were difficult times. I was petrified that they would discover Nicolas was a Jew, even though their papers had been made to disappear, even though our village had always protected them. I don't know what took hold of me. I was young. I was angry—I'd have thrown that bottle against myself if I could have done. I had never heard an explosion before then. There was a flash, then that sound that I seem to hear even today, in moments of silence."

"Every night I wondered what would have happened if I hadn't told Nicolas to move from the water mill to the caves," I said. "I shouldn't have had to make such an important decision."

"After he disappeared, I went back to the mill to look for something, a letter, some page he had underlined in a book. Anything he had left his mark on. When I arrived, I found everything upside down. It was just as you had said—the place wasn't safe.

I'm the only one to blame. If I hadn't thrown the petrol bomb, none of the rest would have happened."

She pushed the chair slightly back from the table, then moved to get up.

"Have you no more time?" I asked.

"I have the children to collect."

She touched the table, still uncertain whether to leave or to remain.

But I could find no words to hold her back. I wanted to ask her about Nicolas, whether she knew what had happened to him, whether she had seen him. Was she right? Had I gone looking for her to talk about him?

A WEEK LATER I RECEIVED A LETTER FROM TERESA. OUR mutual friend must have given her my address.

> *I'm writing to say there's still something I must tell you. But I'll contact you. Don't go searching for me. Don't mention me anymore in your shows. If you must do, then use my real name.*
>
> *I don't like the person you met the other day either. I sometimes feel that life has disfigured me. Yet it was good to find you the same as you were. You've kept that inner strength that I saw from the very first day. You've given it a purpose, but you already had everything inside.*

he show was just a few days away. I spent the morning rehearsing at the theater. I drew chalk lines on the stage, ending up with a series of rectangles, in each of which a part of the monologue would be performed. They represented different places, some more forbidding than others. I had learned, on that evening when I saw the actors at the festa at Tora, that when you're alone in front of an audience, everything counts. If the stage is your world, then you need to know its regions, its cities, its streets.

During the rehearsals I used to ask everyone to leave and, once alone, I would walk along the boards of the stage, sometimes pressing them with my hands to hear whether they creaked. It was another of my practices that had contributed toward my reputation as an actor who was meticulous and disagreeable. I didn't mind being thought of as a rather unsociable character: It helped confirm my own attitude and helped stir the curiosity of the audience.

I had pursued the most ambitious and unattainable desire—to be someone else.

ON ONE OF THE LAST DAYS BEFORE THE SHOW, I CHANGED my route to the theater. I needed a brisk walk to order my thoughts and ended up near Piazza Mercato, where people were hurrying between the stalls. I recognized one voice among the traders that I would never forget. The truck was still the same, older, but clean and polished around its curved metal body. His sales patter had lost none of its vigor, and among the other traders he seemed like an indefatigable lion. I moved closer. Broomsticks, tongs, pliers, rubber seals for coffee pots. Other more up-to-date objects had replaced his old favorites, and the contents of his truck had adapted to more modern needs.

"All American, come ladies and gentlemen, all original American products. Buy these objects just once, and you'll have them for the rest of your lives."

The technique was still the same, he tried to draw the attention of each potential customer. Don Aniello Panzer was a hand-to-hand salesman.

"And wouldn't this young lady like to take a fine American skillet back home with her? What better way to impress your husband? Such a pretty *miss* must surely have a husband or a boyfriend, no? At least two, I'd say."

"Don Aniè, you're always the same," the woman said.

Don Aniello Panzer planted a kiss in the palm of his hand and blew it at the woman.

"And this is for the finest beauty in the market."

I moved closer.

"Do you sell notebooks?" I asked.

I hoped he would recognize me and would ask what had happened since the day he had brought me to Naples.

"I have notebooks, set squares, compasses, pencils, sketchbooks, paintbrushes, watercolors, whatever you wish, *dottò*. They're all there. How many do you want?"

I looked at the pile.

"I'd like ten," I said.

"All these notebooks, and what are you going to write?"

"They're not for me but for a young boy," I replied.

I handed him the money.

"Choose them yourself, *dottò*. Pick whichever takes your fancy."

Meanwhile, a woman passed.

"And wouldn't you like to take an American hair curler home with you? Just think how happy your husband would be. No, impossible that such a beautiful *miss* isn't married. Not even a boyfriend?"

THE STAGE LIGHTS CAME ON, AND I APPEARED. THE AUdience applauded. I moved swiftly to the front of the stage and recited my first line: "I'm sorry to announce that tonight's performance has been canceled. The ticket office will give you a full refund. There's been a problem, and I prefer to tell you myself. I'm very sorry, but you'll get your money back. Please accept my apologies."

I signaled to the technician to raise the lights in the circle. Several people got up, took their coats, and amid the general disappointment began to move toward the exit. I waited until the first of them had reached the last row of seats, then continued. "In any event," I said, "you'd have been bored. The actor would have insulted you. You know what he's like. You can't even imagine how grudging people can be, and I tell you quite honestly, you were taking quite a risk when you bought your ticket."

Several stopped, unsure whether to leave or return to their seats.

"The show has started, then?" asked a man who was still holding his jacket.

"When I return home each evening, I always wonder whether it has finished," I replied.

I put my hands in front of my eyes and kept them covered. I slowly closed my fingers to create two circles. Binoculars. I looked at everyone. Then I moved my hands and put one in front of the other, closed one eye, and peered into what had become a telescope.

I pointed it toward the boxes in the upper tier, then between the front rows, and in the small circle of flesh I saw Teresa. The houselights were still on. One of the two men seated to her right or to her left must have been her husband. I broke the telescope with an elaborate movement of my fingers.

"I'd say we can start."

On that cue the lights dimmed, and the pigs appeared onstage. They were electrically powered and moved along a track. They had little lights instead of eyes and could move their heads from left to right. They seemed to have lives of their own.

I came out with my usual lines. The audience laughed, and anyone would have said it was going well. But the words were not as incisive as I had imagined. The show wasn't very good. It had been a mistake to put it on.

Halfway through, I was supposed to leave the stage for a few minutes. There was a scene of my death by firing squad, and while the pigs moved along the tracks, the sound of the "Lacrimosa" from Mozart's *Requiem* came from the loudspeakers to simulate my funeral and my improbable ascent to heaven.

I went to my dressing room and put a towel over my face. I thought about the pointlessness of all those words I had spoken up to then, and those that still awaited me. I could hear the sound of Mozart and knew there wasn't long before I had to be back onstage.

An attendant knocked on the dressing room door. He had a note in his hand.

"I've been given this for you. It's urgent. I'm sorry, I know you don't like being disturbed, but the person is very insistent."

I took the note and read it. I could hardly breathe.

Now is the winter of our discontent, made glorious summer by this sun of York; and all the clouds that lour'd upon our house, in the deep bosom of the ocean buried. This is the passage that 245 repeated by heart. The only time I spoke to him, he said he would disappear forever to the place with the name of the book. I thought a great deal about these words, the place with the name of the book, but I can't work it out. I hope this might help you. Perhaps he's the man you are looking for.

There were three digits just below: 149. Unbelievable. It was the signature of the woman I had spoken to at the theater in Rome.

I felt a sharp pang and, at the same time, a deep joy. Only Nicolas could have recited those lines, and I now knew beyond doubt where he had gone to disappear. He was in Tora, the place with the name of the book, the Torah. He was alive, just like all of us at that very moment. Just like Teresa, who was sitting by her husband in the front row.

I went back onstage. I didn't want any thought of Nicolas to carry me off track, and I tried to banish him to the edge of my mind, or at least out of the script. The audience laughed at every joke or protested over those more savage remarks where they felt insulted. I was doing better.

I couldn't wait for it to end.

Part Three

THE BALLERINA ON THE TIN BOX

I slipped a few clothes and fresh notebooks into my bag: suitable luggage for a short stay or for disappearing for good. It was perhaps the single advantage of being alone—I could leave the city without telling anyone, a lightness that on some nights dragged me down.

I took my seat in one of the last cars and chose to face backward as if to remind me that I would be returning to Naples.

I noted a few details: the light blue dress of a woman reading a newspaper, the sign warning people not to lean out of the window, the accent of the man who moved between the cars with a wicker basket selling rolls with homemade salami wrapped in brown paper.

I was the only one to leave the train at Tora-Presenzano. In the ticket office, a single clerk sat studying the timetable as if it were a great work of art. I thought of the day when Teresa, Nicolas, and I sat on the low wall with our hair still damp. I shut my eyes for a moment to hear our voices, then picked up my suitcase.

When I went out into the station forecourt, a man came straight toward me.

"Do you need a lift?" he asked. "I can take you wherever you want. Give me the bag, *dottò*. No need to worry."

I handed it to him.

He opened the trunk of his car and put it inside.

"Where can I take you?"

"I'm looking for somewhere to sleep," I said.

"A hotel?"

"Anything will do."

"There's not much choice around here. There's a restaurant just outside the village with rooms upstairs. It's like a small guesthouse if that's all right. It's clean and the owners are nice." He paused to look at my clothes. "Or maybe it's not what you're looking for. We can drive toward Caserta if you prefer. We'll find something better there."

"No, if it's close to the village, that'll be fine," I said.

"You can reach it on foot."

Large black clouds gathered as we drove from the station. The air was close.

"Are you staying long?" the taxi driver asked.

"I don't know yet."

"We don't get many visitors here. Outsiders don't stay long. They come just to see the Ciampate del Diavolo. May I ask if that's why you're here?"

"I'm not sure what you're referring to," I lied. "What is it?"

"The Devil's Footsteps. They say the devil once came down to Tora. If you go to the village, you're sure to find someone who will take you there."

"And why would the devil come to a village as small as this?" I asked, hoping to encourage him.

"Le Ciampate are bare rocks, an expanse of solidified lava on which there are footsteps. No man could have walked on red-hot lava unless he was the devil. And then you see it from the perfection of the cloven foot. If you go, I'm sure you will change your mind."

I turned the handle to open the window.

"It's just a legend, but in the village we're proud of it," the taxi driver continued. "It's not like the city. Here, nothing ever happens, and when there's a story to tell, we end up telling it forever."

The taxi had a smell of fruit, which must have been transported not long before.

"The devil never comes for nothing. He moves around only for a specific purpose," I said.

"And whatever it is, there must be a reason, for sure. We know so little about what goes on. We know only what we see. We think that's everything, and in fact it's only the tiniest part. The devil is what we don't see: the things we invent."

"I like your theory."

"You're very kind. If I say things like that to people in the village, they reckon I'm an idiot, but I can talk to someone like you. Just think, a long time ago, in an out-of-the-way place like this, while the war was still on, they sent Jews here."

"And why send them here? I mean, why not somewhere else?"

"It's the same question as before. Why did the devil decide to come and walk here rather than somewhere else? Things happen, and that's all. If we keep on asking too many questions, we then invent the answers, and the answers become history. The old villagers were afraid the devil would come back, so they saw everything as an omen."

"What happened to the Jews who were sent here?" I asked.

The taxi driver thought for a moment. "They went back to

Naples—some earlier, some later. They were people who'd had everything taken from them. It could happen to anyone. It depends on which side of the road you're born. But when it came to hiding them, nobody here thought twice. It's a small thing, and at the same time a very great thing, if you think about it."

I sat back against the seat. "You must be proud of what you did," I said.

"You can smoke if you wish. I don't mind."

"I don't smoke, thank you," I replied. "And do you remember any of those Jews in particular? I mean, was there anyone who left their mark on the village?"

"Only the devil left his mark. The others were normal people like us, as I told you."

"Yes, you're right. But in certain moments of desperation, normal people can sometimes act in exceptional ways. Desperation is underestimated."

"You certainly know how to talk. Are you from Naples, may I ask? It's hard to say, from the way you speak."

"I live in Naples but came from a small village like this one," I said.

"Small villages are all the same."

There was a moment of silence. As we drove closer, outside the village in an area I hardly recognized, I felt a growing tension and excitement. Returning to the place where I was born, and where I grew up, was the most difficult journey I could imagine.

"Can I ask one last thing?"

"Go ahead," he replied.

"Are you the only taxi driver in the area?"

"I do it to earn a few lire. I go there when the Naples train arrives. I sometimes pick up a respectable customer like you. They're nearly all farmers in the village. I'm the only one with a new car, so I've set myself up in business. And you've noticed how well I keep it? I wash it every week."

"Do you recall whether anyone has arrived recently?"

"There aren't any new people here. We all know each other, and if I may say so, the only new face is yours." The car slowed down. "Here, we've arrived," he said.

It was a small house with a front garden and gravel driveway. I had been past several times when I was a child, though my recollection was vague. It must have been recently renovated.

"There's nothing else here," the man explained. "You'll have to make do. There's a simple restaurant downstairs, bedrooms above. They don't charge much. If you wait here, I'll go and ask the owner if they can take you. Not that they're full—no one ever comes here—but we always need to ask. Otherwise we can go somewhere else."

I got out of the car and waited, leaning against the hood. The metal was hot. I imagined he wanted to talk alone with the owner to collect his tip, having brought her a guest. I looked around. I could get to the village in forty minutes by following the road and maybe cutting through the fields.

"Come," the taxi driver said. "Their rooms are all vacant."

I paid him, and we said goodbye.

I listened to the wheels on the gravel and watched the car return to the road. A young woman meanwhile appeared. She was perhaps a few years older than me and was drying her hands on her apron.

"I'm sorry," she said, "I was in the kitchen. I'm sure Luigi will have filled your head with gossip. He thinks everyone he meets will be interested in his stories. How long will you be staying?"

"I don't know yet," I replied. "If it's all right with you, I can start by paying three days in advance. I don't think I'll be staying any longer."

"Don't worry about money. I asked only to work out which room to give you. I'll have the room looking onto the courtyard prepared for you since you'll be here for more than a night. It's airier. There's not much to see, but you'll get the morning light. That's all we can offer around here."

"All right," I said.

"Will you be stopping for lunch and dinner?"

"I hadn't thought about that."

"You can tell me later. But there aren't many places to eat around here."

"You're right, so I'll stay for dinner. I generally eat just once a day."

The few rooms had no numbers. I was given the one at the end of the corridor.

The woman went to open the French window onto the balcony.

"Have you had other guests recently?" I asked hesitantly.

"People are leaving here. They don't arrive. We had some people from Capua who came to sell land. Then there were some laborers for a construction site near the railway. I'll leave you now. If you need anything, you'll find me in the kitchen."

Once alone, I went out onto the balcony. There were fields and derelict stone houses, and Tora e Piccilli was visible in the distance. It was strange that the place didn't feel familiar. In a certain way, my time in Naples seemed the only life I had had.

I lay down on the bed without taking off my shoes. I didn't notice the approaching tiredness. I shut my eyes and fell asleep.

ince the time I left the village many years before, there were certain questions about my family that I had never really asked. My father, my mother, and my sister had so seldom come to mind that the thought of them had become an inextricable part of those places. In one of my stage monologues, I would talk about a pain I felt between my ribs each time I mentioned my sister. At that time, any mention of the family was taboo, unless you spoke with respect. And yet the family and pain were naturally linked. It could even be suggested it was a pain that ran deeper than any other. I stood at the center of the stage, and each time I said the word *sister*, I put my hand on my breastbone. By the third time, those sitting in the stalls would all be staring at my hand and waiting for my expression of pain. In the final part of the scene, instead of saying the word *sister*, I would touch my breastbone, replacing the word with the gesture.

I had one for my mother too. I described her as an impassive woman who obeyed her husband's Fascist ravings without even once expressing an opinion of her own. In the piece I had written we watched her as she was being seen by a doctor. She had hardly spoken for days. The doctor asked a few questions about her appetite and her back pains. I imitated her voice and her submissive replies of "No." The audience would laugh at each "No." At the end of the consultation, while the doctor was putting his imaginary instruments back into his imaginary bag, he would say, "The patient has been dead eleven years. What we see is her body, which doesn't have the strength to die." Then the doctor asked the last question: "Signora, do you feel alive?"

"No."

"You've heard. The patient confirms that she is dead."

Laughter from the audience.

The purpose of my short theatrical career at times seemed one of exacting revenge, and now that I was back in the village, I felt pangs of remorse for having been too harsh, for disappearing without ever coming back to see them.

I spent the early part of the afternoon in my room. The bed was comfortable, even if a damp smell came from the walls and now and then I had to open the window. I felt a strange excitement, as if I were preparing for an appointment.

When the sun went down, I left the guesthouse and walked half an hour in the darkness, toward the lights in the distance.

I chose the route that skirted the village. Leaving the main road, I took the path that Teresa and I used to call the Channel when we were young. We would pronounce it in our dialect, which, for me, was now a dead language, just as we who spoke it were dead.

When I entered the wood, I lost all sense of time. With each footstep I heard twigs snap beneath my feet. There was one thing in me that hadn't changed: the courage to walk in the darkness, a characteristic of wild animals, of those who know there's nothing to fear about being alone.

And there before me was the image of what I had pictured for all those years: the old mill. From a distance I saw a light. I stopped ten paces from the door. I was tired. The shoes I was wearing were not right, nor my clothing.

"Nicolas," I called into the darkness.

The sound of his name, shouted into the gloom, made me tremble, as if someone else had spoken it.

I called louder: "Nicolas!"

I went up to the door. It was ajar. I knocked. I called again as I pushed the door open: "Nicolas!"

Inside was an old woman with two children who might have been six or seven, both wrapped in a blanket.

"Don't hurt us," she said. "Leave us alone. We have no money."

The children didn't say a word.

"Good young man, let us stay here, we've nowhere to go, we're good people, and you have the face of good person. The Madonna must bless you."

"I don't want to chase you out," I said.

The old woman's wailing became shriller and more constant. She must have misunderstood my words. I stepped inside. The stink was terrible. I moved closer and pulled a couple of banknotes from my pocket. The old woman held out her hand, took the money, and thrust it between her breasts.

Money was a language that everyone knew. I ran my hand through the hair of one of the children. It seemed like flax.

"Is there no one here apart from you?"

"There's only us, but we've done nothing wrong. We have nowhere else. Otherwise we must sleep in the woods, but there are animals and we're afraid."

"How long have you been here with the children?"

"A month. If the owner comes, we'll leave. The night is cold for sleeping outside."

"And when you came here a month ago, was there no one else?"

"It was all empty."

"And you didn't find anything?"

"Like what?"

"I don't know," I said, "some sign that someone had been here."

"We haven't stolen anything."

"I know you haven't taken anything."

"One thing we did find, but it's worth nothing," she said.

"What?"

"I'll let you see."

The old woman got up. The children stayed covered.

"This," she said.

She handed me an oil lamp.

I recognized it immediately.

It was the lamp that Gioacchino had brought with us that night when Nicolas was wounded.

"It was here already. We don't steal anything."

"All right, keep it. Now it's yours."

I gave her another banknote.

"Thank you, thank you," the old woman said, continually swaying as she bowed. I looked into the whites of the children's eyes, then left the mill.

I felt stupid. Years had passed. What could I have hoped to find?

When I returned to the guesthouse, it was deep into the night. Along the road I had seen no one. A couple of dogs barked from behind a gate, and for the rest of the night I heard only insects.

I resolved to go back to Naples the following day.

"You're here. I didn't hear you leave your room," the guesthouse owner said.

"There's a little sun," I replied.

I was on the balcony along the corridor leading to the bedrooms. There was a wooden table and two chairs. I looked out at the countryside, shading my eyes with my hand.

"Later the sun will reach your window too," she said, tracing its path with her finger. "During this month, it's the brightest room."

"Do you mind if I sit here?" I asked.

"Of course not."

She too was looking at the countryside. She rested her arms on the railing. I studied her back and the line of her legs. She turned toward me, her elbows still on the railing.

"The rooms remain vacant for weeks, and when someone occupies them, the whole house knows it. Would you like breakfast? I can bring it to you."

"That makes me feel guilty. I have to tell you I'll be leaving the room shortly," I said.

"I thought you were staying longer."

"I thought so as well. I hope it won't cause you any problems. I'm ready to pay for the other days too."

"I hope we haven't been the problem."

"Everything's perfect here. It's not you."

"Can I say something? I remember you. I know who you are."

I looked at her more closely.

"May I sit down?" she asked, pointing to the empty chair.

I couldn't guess how old she was. Yesterday I thought she was older than me but now I wasn't so sure. In Naples I had known women less beautiful, but women I considered attractive simply because they were conscious of their own beauty.

"I lived at Conca della Campania. My father had land and owned some rabbits, hens, and a pig that frightened me because it was so big. We bought it from your father at the market. You and I were there that morning, together with our fathers. Then I saw you at other times in the village."

"I'm sorry we sold you a pig that frightened you," I said. "They are trusty and intelligent animals. And I'm sorry not to remember you."

"It doesn't matter. I remember that the pig was fair with dark patches on its back. It was an animal just too big for a little girl who loved rabbits. The thought came back to me while I was looking at you this morning. When you arrived yesterday, I recognized the dialect but still hadn't guessed who you were."

"It's my true language. Each time I need to say something, I think it in our dialect, then translate into Italian or Neapolitan. The truth is that every thought I have passes first through these places, then ends up where I happen to be."

"I haven't seen you since the war—neither you nor your family."

"I work in Naples now," I said. "I don't know where my father and mother are."

"I left too, but I wasn't as clever as you. So here I am." She paused. "You don't have any relatives to ask? People can't just disappear like that."

"I could perhaps ask. There are people I could ask. Yes, I will ask."

"The truth is that families are dangerous places. No one ever says that."

I thought it would be a good line for a monologue.

Question: Do you know the most dangerous place I've been to in the past few years? Answer: My family.

"But the pigs have been back for some time," she added.

"What do you mean?"

"Yes, for some time."

"And who looks after them?"

"You never see him in the village. Every so often he comes to the square with the child to do some shopping. He's a strange type, never talks to anyone. No one is sure he's even Italian."

I remained silent, feeling the sun on my face.

"And why did you return?" I asked her, with my eyes closed.

"I told my family I was going to live with a girlfriend, but well—I don't know how to say it. We weren't just friends." She sniffed deeply, then leaned back against the chair. "It's the first time I've said that."

"To strangers you can say anything."

"It feels good to say it."

We sat silently in the sun, both of us probably thinking about what we had gained from that conversation.

"Well, I must go back to the restaurant. The workers from the construction site are arriving later, and everything must be ready. Leave the keys in the lock when you go. I hope all goes well."

I went to the room for the last time, brushed my teeth and washed my face with cold water, then left the keys as she had asked.

I had jotted the train times in my notebook. There would be two for Naples Central that morning. I took the same road as the day before, but carrying the suitcase that identified me as a stranger wherever I went. I took the path that led to my parents' house. The trees were an element of continuity in a world that had completely changed.

As I drew nearer, I felt a sensation that both attracted and repelled me, and when I saw the house I stopped, unable to proceed. Objects outside confirmed that life went on: a wheelbarrow, a bucket, chopped wood, clothes out to dry on the line. Someone was living there.

"Good morning," I called out.

I tried again, immediately.

"Is anyone there?"

Then I saw him.

He came out of the pigsty dressed in rags. Arms like vine stems. His long hair partly over his eyes, beard untrimmed, ribs sticking out.

When I called his name, he turned and looked at me.

It seemed impossible that he and I could have exchanged roles. He was living in what was once my house, the new pig keeper, the new village idiot. Without him, the person who had just walked out of the sty on that sunny morning would have been me.

"Nicolas, it's me, Davide," I said.

He made the only gesture he could possibly make. He slowly

opened his arms and stood where he was, as if to display his nakedness. I went toward him, my eyes filled with tears. As I embraced him, I felt the labyrinth of bones around his back and chest. He had given me a new life, whereas my legacy to him was the stink of pigs that hung in his hair and in his beard. These were the gifts we had given each other. He had saved me, but what was my gift to him? He stood motionless with his arms at his sides. I didn't yet know that he lacked the strength to hold me tight. His muscles were strong enough to carry a tin bucket of animal mash, but not to embrace me.

When he spoke my name, I thought he seemed reluctant to see me and that all my feelings toward him over those years had been just my imagination.

The door of the house opened at that moment, and a young boy came out. He looked like Nicolas, seemed born from his body, a piece that had broken away and taken life.

"Why have you come?" Nicolas asked.

"To find you."

He covered his eyes with his hand. I never knew whether he was ashamed of crying in front of me, or in front of his son, or of crying itself. He couldn't hide the tears that streamed down his face.

"Come," he said. "This is Francesco, my son."

The boy took a step toward me. He stood straight, to let himself be seen as Nicolas had asked.

I bent down and touched his soft pink cheeks. I had never spoken to a child and didn't know what tone of voice to adopt.

"We're not very sociable. We never see anyone," Nicolas said to justify his son's embarrassment. "You look very smart," he added, peering at my clothes, then at the suitcase. "Where were you going?"

"Home," I replied.

Nicolas turned to look back at the house where he lived and the pigsty. He opened his arms.

"Then you've arrived. Stay with us for a while."

EVERYTHING WAS STILL AS IT WAS. I STARED AT THE place where I used to see my mother and sister bent over, chopping vegetables or kneading dough. I still seemed to see Rosetta running along the corridor pulling her rag dog behind her. The photographs of Jesus and Mussolini had gone. Two lighter rectangles on the wall testified to their existence.

"We survive on little," Nicolas explained. "We take what we have from the vegetable patch and from our animals. It's enough for us. I've become pretty smart, not as smart as you were, but I've learned a few things. And then there's the silence, and we can go for walks. Who knows whether such things still interest you."

"I'm sure I'll be fine," I said. I hadn't decided to stay, but the words came out of my mouth unprompted.

We still felt distant. Just as Teresa and I had been. I knew it would take time for us to get to know each other again.

"You could help us out. Maybe you'll need some other clothes."

"I have only these," I said, looking at my trousers.

"They'll get ruined."

"I have more at home. It doesn't matter."

"You're too well dressed to feed pigs. Come, settle yourself in the other room. Francesco and I sleep together. There's the spare room."

I bent down again and held my hand out to the boy.

"Won't you say hello?" I asked.

Francesco didn't move.

"You have to shake his hand," Nicolas said. "Look, it's easy, you have to put your hand in this man's hand and then shake it."

"All right," Francesco said, doing as his father had told him.

I felt his soft little hand in mine.

"Harder," I said.

He gritted his teeth.

"That's better. I'm Davide. I used to live in this house when I was your age. But a long time has passed since then. I'll have to learn everything all over again."

"All right," Francesco said. "I'll show you how to feed the hens without letting them peck you. They're really quick. You have to stand on the rock. They can't jump up there, so you're safe."

We walked along the corridor to the room where I slept as a child. It was empty apart from the old wardrobe and a mattress covered with dust.

"We'll open the window for a while," Nicolas said. "Where have you come from?"

"Naples."

He looked me up and down.

"I always thought you and that city had something in common. It's a place where everyone has their own way of living. You'd have found it easy to remain there."

"I took without giving," I said.

"For other people it's the opposite. What happened to your leg?"

I did a turn around the room to show him how my movement had improved.

"I had an operation. It's a fairly common defect. If I were still cooped up here, I would never have known."

"I find you different in everything . . ."

"It's just the clothes. If you put me in a pigsty, I'm just the same person."

"I'll make some lentil soup, then I have to go to the vegetable patch."

"I'll give you a hand."

"You'll be the best-dressed farmer that Tora e Piccilli has ever had."

We both laughed. Now I seemed to recognize the voice of the boy who recited "the deep bosom of the ocean."

"I've cleared a patch of land nearby and go each day to work it. That piece of land has been generous to me. You'll taste an excellent soup."

He closed the door as he went out. I lay on the bed without undressing. The base was hard, the mattress had no recollection of my body. But as soon as I stretched out, I seemed to lay myself over my own ghost, as if I were filling a shell that had been waiting motionless for me for years.

woke. No sounds came from the house, and I wasn't sure what time it was. When I went into the kitchen, I found Nicolas sitting and reading.

"You've woken up. I hope we didn't make a noise," he said.

"I slept the whole afternoon. In the place where I live, you hear people shouting at all hours. I'm not used to such silence anymore."

"Silence has a texture here. You can almost touch it. But you already know these things." He looked at the pots in the sink. "Are you hungry?"

"Yes."

"I'll warm supper."

I sat down in the kitchen and watched Nicolas stir something on the fire.

"It's delicious," I said after I had tasted it, and I thought it really was. It was a soup with potatoes, peas, and lentils. He stayed in the kitchen to watch me eat, just a few steps away. I dipped a spoon into the dish and filled it with warm soup.

"Your father?" I asked.

I didn't know how to finish the sentence.

Nicolas parted his lips without making a sound, as if he had tried but failed.

"He went to join my mother and my sisters in Turin. He wrote poetry and continued to give private lessons but didn't go back to school. He died three years ago. He'd always had a weak heart. He used to say everyone was born with some defect, and that was his. Last time we met, we spoke about you."

He gazed at the sink.

"I have no words to tell you what I feel," I said.

"There's no need to say anything."

Nicolas went to the window. It was dark. No lights were visible in the distance. In the silence, crickets and cicadas could be heard.

"Once in Rome I saw a playbill for a show, with your name and your face," he said.

"You were in Rome?"

"At a certain point in my complicated journey, yes."

"I'd like to know about it," I said.

He glanced at the door, unconsciously searching for Francesco. Then he began, as if continuing an unfinished conversation: "When I realized the Germans were in the woods, I left the cave and ran off. I lost my way among the trees, went around in circles for a day, then finally I reached a road. I found a truck there and managed to get to Rome. I didn't yet know what to do. My father was at Tora, and I had no idea how to contact him. We had talked about it. In the event of danger, we were to save ourselves first, then look for the other. I thought of going to our relatives in the north, where my mother and sister had been for some time, but the next day they caught me. They put me on a train . . ." Here he stopped for a few moments. Then he continued. "After that, I couldn't go back to Naples, so I stayed in Rome for a while. I would have preferred to die like all the others, as I should have done. I've asked myself hundreds of times: Why not me? How is it decided?"

I didn't know how to answer. Instead, I asked him, "When you saw the playbill for my show, why didn't you try looking for me?"

He went quiet. I had asked the wrong question.

"Too much time had gone by. I wasn't sure you'd want to see me again. And then, what Nicolas would you have met? There's nothing left of the one we used to know."

"Did Teresa have anything to do with your decision not to see me again?"

He looked up at the ceiling. That name still produced a reaction in both of us.

Francesco came into the kitchen at that moment, wrapped in a blanket.

Nicolas took him in his arms.

"Can't you sleep?"

"No."

"Are you afraid?"

"No."

"Do you want me to come with you?"

Francesco nodded then whispered something in his ear.

"All right, we'll say good night. Say good night to Davide."

"Good night," Francesco said.

"Tomorrow morning I'm going to the vegetable patch. Francesco comes with me. If you want to join us when you wake up, just follow the path. There's a redbrick house. Carry on walking, you'll find us further on. I'll leave you some more suitable clothes."

ONCE ALONE IN THE KITCHEN I HAD TO ADMIT THAT Nicolas's good looks, which had so affected me on the day he arrived in Tora, had now gone. It was a minor consideration after all that had happened to him, but I couldn't get it out of my mind. I had found them again in his son's eyes, though that gift also seemed to hold a darker aspect that I could now see for the first time.

I went to the pigsty. I was familiar with the smell of dung and of the animals. There were just four of them, all at the far end of the sty, lying on the straw. The fences had gone. The drinking troughs were full, and so too were the buckets from which they fed. Nicolas was taking good care of them. When they noticed I was there, they kept me in their sight. They struggled to their feet and moved closer together, into a compact group, ready to defend themselves or to attack. I went up to the wooden gate and held my hand out to touch one of them. The pig was nervous. It moved its head up and down, preparing its back muscles for the impact but finally let itself be touched. I remembered Nero, his beauty, and his strength.

THE NEXT MORNING I WENT TO THE VEGETABLE PATCH. Nicolas had left some clothes folded on the chair. They must have been ones he usually wore, and when I fastened the last button, I realized they had been mine when I lived there. I walked along the path he had described. It had rained during the night, and the grass on each side was wet. After walking for a few minutes, my shoes had forgotten the paved roads and had surrendered to the earth and to the water. Then I saw them.

Nicolas was bent over the soil, while Francesco ran around the field chasing something.

"We're here," Nicolas shouted, waving his hand.

I looked at his scrawny arm held up in the air. I moved toward them.

"Your shoes are already ruined," he said as I approached.

"It doesn't matter. I never liked them."

"Nor do I, though I didn't want to say it yesterday," and we laughed for the second time since we'd met.

"This is your bucket," he said, pointing to it.

"What do I have to do?"

"You really have forgotten everything. Well then, you go behind me. We'll work back-to-back. You take the peas, pick them off close to the stem, like this, so as not to damage the plant, then put them in the bucket. Leave the ones that are too small. They'll have to be left for another week. When we get home, we'll feed the pigs."

"I remember how that's done."

"You can do it, then."

"All right. And the hens?" I asked with a smile.

"Francesco does that. He has a name for them all. His favor ite is Ulla. She has red feathers, and every day he goes to see if there are any chicks."

"What kind of name is Ulla?"

"He's a child with a great imagination, so unlike me. You've no idea how happy I am."

"He likes it here," I said.

"This is a holiday for him. He loves doing little jobs. Everything's a game for him. He'll soon be going home, though."

We moved slowly. I had done it as a child, with my father. It was he who used to look after the vegetable patch. I enjoyed it. We would leave early in the morning and walk into the fields, making the dogs bark. He used to make a noise with his mouth, and the dogs would stop. Then something broke between us.

Nicolas held the stems to feel their firmness, and when the plants had given their approval, he moved toward the pods.

"I saw Teresa in Rome," he said. "I didn't know whether I could say it yesterday, but now I think we can talk without hurting each other."

His voice was calm, each movement measured. I was on the point of telling him I had seen her again a few days before my departure for Tora e Piccilli, but I hesitated, and the moment passed forever.

"It was she who found me," he continued. "I was living at the house of Luisa, a friend of mine from Naples who has been in Rome for many years. I didn't know where to go, Luisa had a spare room, and she told me I could stay as long as I had to. I didn't tell her where I had been. She realized there was something I didn't want to talk about, and she asked no questions. She found me some work with a florist. I did the deliveries."

He looked at the peas that he held tightly between his hands.

"The scent from the greenhouse that you entered through a small inner door . . . that was what saved me. It was then that I began to think about coming back here. I don't know how Teresa managed to find me, but from then on, she took care of me so far as I allowed her. I moved into her house, and there I met her son, Antonio. An intelligent and determined child, he treated me with suspicion. He called me Signor Nicolas at first. After a few months, when Teresa told me she was pregnant, I asked her to get rid of it, but she wouldn't listen. And now he's there chasing crows, the child who thinks up names for the hens."

He turned to look at him.

"There's nothing I love more on this earth. But after he was born, my nightmares returned. Once more, I couldn't eat or sleep." We remained silent. Then he added: "Before seeing Teresa again, I was convinced it was you who had betrayed me. For a long time I felt a hatred toward you."

He spoke without looking at me. We continued moving back-to-back. I turned once more toward Francesco, who was tossing pebbles over a low stone wall.

"Teresa told me that you'd hidden me in the cave because it was safer, that I shouldn't be angry with you. I thought, after what I had experienced, that I was ready for anything, and yet I still felt jealous over a woman. I was still alive."

"I would never have hurt you," I said.

"The truth is that if I hadn't come to Tora, you and Teresa would have had a different life."

"You've been the most important person in my life." I managed to say those words with no feeling of shame.

Then he had a coughing fit. He put his hands to his chest. I saw his lungs heaving in and out.

"Go to Francesco," he said, between one attack and another.

I moved toward him, but he pushed me away, still pointing at the child.

"It will soon pass."

His coughing affected his whole chest, causing him to shake. During the few moments of respite, he was wheezing and gasping for breath. When the attack began to subside, Nicolas lay on the ground between the two rows of peas and dug his fingers into the soil. At that moment I understood his wish to die, to mingle with the soil and turn himself into roots. He wasn't the special being I had dreamed about, but a fragile man scarred by a wound that would never leave him. When he spoke again, his voice was calm once more.

"I was sick. Too sick. I left Teresa's house and took a room for myself. Teresa and the two children came to see me. She managed to explain to them why we didn't live together anymore. I told her I wanted to cut myself off from the world. I wanted to cultivate the land, to keep animals. I wanted to become a woodland animal like you were. And so I returned. It seemed the only place possible. The village had accepted me at one time, and I knew it would continue to do so. Teresa came to see me for a few days with the children. She wanted me and Francesco to spend time together, but now she has her hospital life and a husband who gives her peace of mind."

He got his breath back. His story was putting everything into place.

"My days with Francesco are magnificent. The universe seems to have another meaning, but everything's coming to an end. Francesco will soon be going back to his mother forever. I haven't yet told Teresa."

I looked him in the eyes to understand what he meant.

"I'm dying. I have cancer, and it can't be treated. I want to live what I have left far away from humanity. I prefer the bounty of this vegetable patch, the pride of oaks, the dignity of crows. It's a great privilege to have Francesco with me over these last days. And now you're here too."

"We'll go and see a doctor. We need to get away from Tora. No one here can do anything for you."

"No, it's too late. I've had much more time than so many boys who were taken to the camp. Every day I waited my turn, and now it's coming."

He seemed to be staring at the clouds.

"Help me get up, Davide."

It was only when he gripped my arm to stand up again that I felt just how little his body weighed.

 stopped counting the days I spent at Tora. The clothes that Nicolas gave me were now mine again, and our lives merged once more, as they had at the beginning, when in the village he knew only me.

One day I took Francesco to the stream and taught him to catch frogs. We plunged into the cold expanse of water, and at that moment I realized that somewhere that boy I used to be, the one who had grown up in the countryside, still existed. I still knew how to walk barefoot on the stones that lay on the bottom of the stream without slipping or falling. From the time Nicolas told me about his illness, I devoted myself to small things, to a day at a time—shopping to do in the village, something to pick in the vegetable patch, animals to feed, or a new story to make up for Francesco. I had decided neither to stay nor to leave and, more generally, I still didn't know what to do about my life and about the theater. I felt that Nicolas continued to influence me with his purity, and his illness somehow increased his luminosity. His mystery still seemed unfathomable, and every attempt to explain it was a simplification. I had imitated him but had never equaled him. Everything he told me bore deeply into me. The imminence of his death and the lucidity with which he faced it were beyond my grasp.

We spent the days following age-old patterns linked to the earth and to animals. Francesco was the hinge around which everything turned. He was given the easier tasks, which he performed with great responsibility. Nicolas had told him he would soon be setting off on a journey, that he would be away for a long time but would find some way to appear and to make himself heard. When Francesco asked if one day they would see each other again, Nicolas said that journeys were in a single direction and people never go back to the same place because everything changes, and we need to accept the transformation.

As the days passed, Nicolas's powers waned. The heavier jobs were for me, and I did them effortlessly. Nicolas kept a kind of house calendar. There were the dates when beans, peas, and lentils were to be planted and when they were to be picked. There were instructions we would have to follow when he was no longer able to talk. It seemed as if, behind the disorder of my life, a preestablished order was emerging. As if everything were governed by a specific law and Nicolas had the ability to reveal it from the very start.

He had also drawn a map of the neighboring properties. I had to admit he was an excellent cartographer. There was the path that led to the village in one direction and toward the mountain in the other. Everything abandoned by families like mine who used to live in the countryside had been taken under his protection.

Any other person in his condition would have done no more than rest, to ease the strain on his body and fight the spread of the disease. Nicolas had decided instead that everything had to end as soon as possible.

The organization of the pigsty was different from the way I had done it as a boy. With no fencing, the space was more efficiently used, and the animals could move about. They too had established rules for themselves, and I learned their hierarchy. The one in charge was a female. Nicolas had repaired the drinking and feeding troughs. The small grain store at the back of the sty had been cleaned out. This was another part of his legacy: to leave everything in order. To leave it better than he had found it.

ONE AFTERNOON I WENT OUT ALONE. NICOLAS HAD BEEN ill during the morning, and after the pain had passed, he decided to stay at home with Francesco. So I took the map and went out. I followed the routes he had drawn.

I wrote down a few notes. Using Nicolas's map made me realize that my relationship with the theater was not yet over, that I could explore new avenues. I seemed to have caught a fever. I reached a meadow I had never seen before. I found a small wooden hut built on the side of a large rock that had protected it from bad weather over the years. There was a cot and a table inside. If only I could keep my ideas as tidily as that shepherd who had managed to make do with the essential.

I spent the night in the shelter. There was total darkness. The wolves in the distance sniffed my scent, and each passed their fervor to the other. I ate a piece of bread I had brought with me and let everything be filled by the darkness and the silence. All was distant, all was close.

With the first light of dawn, I set off. The night is a blessing for plants. The grass was wet. Along the way I came across the carcass of an animal torn apart by wolves.

I followed the map in the opposite direction and imagined Nicolas alone in those places as he estimated the distance traveled on foot and could then draw the new area on the paper I was holding in my hands.

I went to the field where I knew I would find them. Francesco left Nicolas and ran up to me.

"Davide," he shouted, and he hugged me. I felt his warm, light body. His fear had melted. He was happy to see me.

Nicolas watched the scene.

"I won't go off again at night," I told Francesco.

EACH MORNING I WENT EARLY INTO THE FIELDS. NICOLAS wanted Francesco to come with me. We were out for many hours, often until lunchtime. I took a blanket and let him keep it around his shoulders until the sun was high, then he would start running between the rows of potatoes.

"Can I do it too?" he asked me one morning.

"What?"

"What you are doing."

"But it's no fun. I'm gathering potatoes. You carry on playing."

"I want to do it too."

In those moments I could see Teresa's character in him, the same stubbornness she displayed with the workers at her father's ropeworks when she wanted to be involved in the work.

"All right, you take some too and put them in this bucket. Shall I show you how it's done? You pull up the plant, and then you start digging right there under where you've pulled."

"But there are too many."

"We'll leave some in the pigsty. We'll take them into the house a few at a time."

Francesco dug the ground with a stick I had found for him and gave a laugh with each potato that appeared, as if he had found a gold nugget.

"Shall we take mine home and leave yours here?"

"All right. Keep them separate from the ones I collect. We'll just take yours."

As his potatoes were piling up, I had the chance to ask him a few questions. He displayed a knowledge of the language beyond that of a six-year-old, as well as an accuracy in his observations. I would have recognized Nicolas's son in him just by hearing him speak.

"Count how many potatoes you have," I said.

"Thirty-nine."

"The bucket can hold twenty-six. How many do we have to leave out?"

"Thirteen. But that's not true You can get at least sixty in the bucket."

We set off for the house, but when he tried to lift the handle, he realized it was too heavy, so I carried it. He took hold of it when we reached the door.

"Look, *papà*. These are what I collected."

Nicolas wasn't in the kitchen as he generally was at that time. I went looking for him in the bedroom and found him lying unconscious on the floor.

Francesco dropped the bucket, and the potatoes rolled like misshapen marbles around our feet.

I felt Nicolas's face, his neck, his hands. He opened his eyes, then spoke Francesco's name and mine.

IT WOULD ALL HAVE BEEN SIMPLER IF WE HAD GONE back to Naples and been assisted by a doctor, but Nicolas's wishes were clear.

That evening I put in order the notes I had been jotting down in the fields each morning or during the hours I spent in the pigsty. Sometimes I would read aloud to my little audience what I had written down. We were in Nicolas's bedroom. I'd rest my back against the wall and, before speaking, would always make a gesture with my hands, as if I needed to take a run-up. Francesco laughed each time, and each time, for this reason, I tried to make it last a few seconds longer. I told stories about the potatoes, about the beans, about the beehive near the oak trees, and the colony of ants that went into the hole in our vegetable patch and down to the center of the earth inhabited by prehistoric ants who could talk. I recited the prayer that the bees had written for their queen.

"Do bees really have a queen? Does she have a crown?"

Nicolas spent almost the whole day in bed.

"When I'm better, I will do everything myself, and I'll look after you like queen bees," he said, but we both knew, after the last crisis, that we had passed the point of no return.

On some mornings in the fields, Francesco would repeat some of the lines I had performed the previous evening. When I told Nicolas about this, he laughed.

"I'm pleased he's known you. It might not have happened," he said one day. "When I came here, the people in the village thought it was you who had returned. They thought the only possible pig keeper in this village was you. Some old man called me by your name, and I turned away." He then grew serious. "Listen, Davide, when it happens, I want you to bury me in the fields. On the map I've drawn a rectangle. You'll find it at the end of the path before it starts to climb. In the summer there's plenty of shade, and in the winter the trees protect it from the rain and the wind. There's to be no cross, no stone, no inscription. Don't write my name. Wrap my body in a piece of cloth and bury me with that. Do it so that the roots of a tree can touch my arms. Do it so that in ten years I'm turned into a tree. And lastly, do it so that our children stay united and know that the fates of their fathers crossed each other. Tell them this story."

"I will never have a child," I said.

Nicolas fixed his eyes on me.

"Antonio, Teresa's son, is yours. When I saw him, Teresa didn't need to explain anything else. He's so much like you."

"I don't understand," I said, bewildered.

Nicolas cleared his throat.

"Well, I mean, I don't need to tell you how it happened."

Even today I sometimes think back over how I heard of Antonio's existence from Nicolas, and how until that moment it had never occurred to me that I might have had a child. I was conditioned by an urge for freedom, a selfishness, but there was also the stormy relationship with my father, so abruptly interrupted that it ruled out the possibility of any pardon. I seemed to have inherited from Furtunà the incapacity to be a father.

In the letter that Teresa wrote a few days after our meeting in Naples, she told me there was another thing she had to tell me. The only possible other thing had to be Antonio. Maybe this was why she hadn't gone looking for me, so that she didn't feel a duty to tell me the truth.

e spent many days waiting for something to happen. I wondered how it would happen and how I would tell Francesco, if the right words existed.

One day while Nicolas was sleeping, I asked Francesco to take a spade. We walked behind the pigsty, and I stopped at an exact spot.

"Here," I said, indicating where to dig.

It was hard for him. Digging required much strength or much motivation, and Francesco had neither. Both of us held the spade and began to inch our way into the soil. The earth was compact and was dug up in clods that were bound together by fine roots that resembled human arteries.

"Carry on. It can't be deep," I said.

After a few more strokes, the spade hit something metallic. We knelt and carried on digging with our hands. The object that emerged was very different from the potatoes Francesco had collected a few days before. It was the ballerina on the tin box.

"How did you know it was here?" Francesco asked.

"I hid it many years ago, for you," I said. "It's a present."

"Did you know we would meet?"

"Yes."

"Then it's true what my father said, that you lived here before us. When you told me, I thought it was a joke."

"Yes, I used to live here."

"Were there pigs and rabbits too?"

"There was everything."

"Also ants?"

"Ants as well."

"Also hens?"

"The parents of Ulla's parents."

Francesco held the soil-encrusted ballerina. He was thrilled by the coldness and firmness of its metal.

"How does it work?" he asked.

"I'll show you."

We went into the house where there was more light. The white rag in which the ballerina was wrapped was caked with soil, and the finer roots had grown through its mesh. I had forgotten the box was so heavy. We looked for a tool to put into the hole to wind it up. Having found one that fit, I heard the spring tighten a couple of turns.

"Now let's see if it still works," I said.

I pulled the false key out of the mechanism, and the ballerina turned twice on herself with a hesitant, shuddering movement, uncertain and amazed that she could use her body once again after all those years spent underground. It was a stupid thought, but I felt she was happy to come back to life. Francesco watched her in awe.

"Can I keep her?"

"She's yours."

A FEW DAYS LATER, FRANCESCO AND I WENT TO THE VILLAGE. It was market day and the first time that he and I had been seen out together. We walked among the stalls, and I bought some sugar-coated candies, which the woman gave me in a paper bag. There was a smell of ground coffee in the air.

"They tickle," he said, putting a candy into his mouth.

I realized that this was another reason why Nicolas wanted me to grow to like Francesco: to prepare me to love Antonio. In the meantime, after he had told me, I had tried to push any thought of Antonio into some deep and inaccessible part of myself. I looked at Francesco and thought how much easier it would be to love a son who was not your own.

Francesco was startled by the people rummaging in baskets of clothes and the sellers shouting what they had in their stall. As we wandered about, we were approached by a heavily built man with metal-rimmed spectacles.

"Are you Davide?"

I looked at him, recognized him, and remembered his family. I had seen his leg bleeding on the church soccer field and had watched the priest organize a small procession.

"I'm Renato. My father had the pharmacy. I work there now."

"I remember," I said.

We shook hands like two strangers.

He had grown fat and was balding. He had become his father. His voice had lost the aggression it once had, and his youthful defiance seemed to have gone. It seemed hardly possible that he could have organized the gang that attacked Nicolas in those early days and that I could have joined him in the hope of being his friend.

"Maybe you can help me," I ventured. "I need something for pain."

"Where exactly is it?"

"I can't be sure, exactly. Do you have something to help you relax?"

"Have you seen a doctor?"

"Sometimes it's really bad."

"I can give you some medication, but I need a prescription."

"I don't have anything. I've got some money, maybe it's not enough. I'll come back later and bring the rest."

"You needn't worry. Come with me."

We went to the pharmacy.

"Wait here. I'll go to the back," Renato said. "I have something that will help you, but be careful not to overuse it."

"I'll be careful," I said. "I'll take it only if necessary."

Francesco was sniffing the air. There was something he found familiar: the aroma of alcohol that you smell in surgeries and hospitals, which he might have recognized on his mother's clothing when she came home from work. Renato returned after a few minutes with two bottles of pills.

"Take two of these if the pain gets bad," he said. "They'll help you relax, but you still need to talk to a doctor."

I shook his hand.

When we got back from the market, we found Nicolas in bed. Blood had trickled from his nose, though he hadn't noticed. The part that was dry had darkened and hardened on the sheets. I told Francesco to stay in the kitchen. I washed Nicolas's face with cold water while he apologized for the situation in which we found ourselves. I gave him two tablets.

He seemed better over the next few days, mysteriously alternating between good days and others that were darker. That slow death brought continual changes of mood.

On evenings when he was better, I carried on with my little

shows for them. It was the least I could do. Nicolas and Francesco were a critical but indulgent audience. They made allowances for my experimentations, for my lapses, but let me know when I was on the right track. Nicolas insisted that Francesco and I should go to the vegetable patch each morning. He desperately wanted to die alone.

The deep bosom of the ocean was now wide open and swallowing us all.

With the painkillers, the situation improved: the general pain of the whole house had lessened, and they also helped Nicolas sleep during the day. I wrote page after page, as if I knew the script by heart, and was already imagining the new squares I would draw on the stage. I would have told the story about those days in a farmhouse waiting for an event full of light without ever naming it, about a little boy who fed a colony of ants, about trees that sang at night as the wind blew through the leaves.

I wrote a letter to Teresa, addressed to the hospital where she worked.

Dear Teresa,

I hope you receive this letter. I'm in Tora, at my parents' house. I'm with Nicolas and Francesco. Nicolas's condition is very serious. He doesn't have much time, a matter of days. The pain will soon carry him away. Francesco is a wonderful child. Come as soon as you can. I would like you to bring Antonio. Nicolas has told me everything. I won't interfere with your life. I'll respect your decision.

Davide

ore days went by, and Nicolas seemed comfortable. He was no longer eating, had lost his appetite, and was now more asleep than awake. He eventually asked to keep the curtains drawn.

He died one afternoon at three, while we were talking. I thought it was a pause in the conversation, and maybe he's still somewhere looking for the reply. The last thing he talked about was my shoes. He was sorry they had been ruined from working in the fields, but in the end that was the best fate for a good pair of handmade shoes. For the last time, I looked at the face that was no longer his, and closed his eyes.

Francesco was outside, busy with the hens. I walked in the fields to release the tension that was still building in my legs. I had no faith, and my experience led me to conclude that everything ended at that precise instant, though this did nothing to diminish the significance of the event.

I returned to the house after an hour's walk, following no particular route, just as he used to do when we were boys at Tora and would go off discovering new places. To imagine the world without him was too painful.

At home, I stretched out in the bathtub and washed myself. I lay in the water, not moving. I was already performing his death scene.

Francesco came into the bathroom, took a wooden stool, and sat by the bathtub. He laid his forehead on my shoulder. His eyes were filled with tears.

Teresa arrived with Antonio the next day. She put a hand to her mouth when she saw Nicolas. Her gasp seemed to spread around the room.

Antonio wasn't the child a few years older than Francesco that I had imagined. He was a man in miniature who wore serious clothes like a clerk in a government ministry. He had a hint of a mustache. His hair was longer at the front and was short, almost shaven, around the ears. His shirt was buttoned to the collar.

"Hello," I said.

"Good morning, Signor Davide," he replied. He knew my name.

I held out my hand, and he shook it. He seemed quite accustomed to that gesture.

Teresa and the boys moved into my room while I set the cot up for myself in the kitchen. She had arrived with a small bag, a leather suitcase that a diplomat might have used for a one-night stay. Perhaps it was her husband's, and most of the things she had brought were for Francesco. Clean shoes, fresh shirts, a light coat. Francesco had a wardrobe full of clean clothes waiting for him in a big city. The child I had known in the countryside would disappear as soon as he was back home, and he would recall those days as marking the end of his childhood.

Being there with Teresa took us back in time. While Francesco took Antonio to see the animals and the fields, Teresa and

I could talk about our childhood days in Tora e Piccilli as children, when I went to the ropeworks and her father didn't want us to be friends, or when she tested her courage by touching the pigs.

"They frightened me, and yet I couldn't resist. I didn't want to be frightened of anything. Nero was enormous, and yes, he scared me," she said. She paused for a moment and looked toward the room where Nicolas still lay, then through the window where Antonio and Francesco could be seen. "I wanted to be the best, the cleverest—first in the village, then in class, then at work. I kept on outdoing everyone until I ended up alone. I've become the most lonesome, so I have won in something."

She opened her hands to indicate that was all. I noted a slight tremor. The nail varnish made them seem those of a woman, yet the chewed nails were like those of a child.

"You're not alone. You have Antonio and Francesco," I said.

THAT MORNING I DUG A RECTANGULAR HOLE IN THE place where Nicolas had indicated. The spade stopped about a meter down, where the soil reached a solid layer of rock.

We left the children at the house and loaded Nicolas's body wrapped in sheets onto the pig cart. We walked in silence along the path, and when we arrived, we lowered him into the pit. Teresa began to cry. She was used to seeing people die but wasn't ready for it to happen to the love of her life.

We recited no prayer. We entrusted him to the earth, as I had done years before with the tin ballerina. We felt the wind brush our faces and breathed the damp smell of the earth.

Over supper I told the children a little story I had made up. Antonio laughed, and at the end all three clapped their hands.

During the night I could hear them talking on the other side of the wall. Francesco was doing the talking, while Antonio listened in silence and said just yes or no.

The next day, Teresa and the boys prepared to leave for Naples. Francesco was almost unrecognizable in his clean clothes and with his hair washed and combed.

"Look after yourself," I said.

I really didn't expect it. I bent down and he came to hug me.

"I'll come to see you when I'm in Naples," I said with my mouth by his neck.

"Come soon, then."

Antonio watched our goodbye without intervening. His upbringing prevented him from butting into other people's conversation. I turned toward him, and we shook hands.

"Bye," I said.

"Goodbye," he replied.

"Did you sleep well?" I asked.

This was my first question to my son. The thought was not as unbearable as I had imagined. Now that he was there in front of me, it seemed something possible.

"I slept well, thank you. The mattress was most comfortable, and the sheets had a fine smell."

It certainly wasn't true that the sheets had a fine smell, but I appreciated his attempt not to embarrass me. I stroked his hair from his forehead. Antonio was just like Furtunà. He had the same eyes, the same jawline.

Teresa stood a few steps away. She saw my hand on Antonio's forehead. She knew she could trust me, and she also knew she couldn't stop me from doing it.

"Let's meet in Naples," I said, holding Antonio's hand in mine.

"Very well, Signor Davide," he replied. "We look forward to your visit."

"I could take you and Francesco one Sunday to the park at the Villa Comunale or the woods at Capodimonte. Do you play soccer?"

"I'm brilliant," Francesco said.

"I was sure of that," I replied.

"We must go now," Teresa said.

She came up, kissed me on the cheek, and after holding her lips there for a moment, she hugged me. I recognized the aroma of her neck and the lightness of her body against mine. The same as that night on which we had made love.

"Don't disappear," she said.

At the station, I helped them onto the train.

I told myself that one day I would find the words to talk to Antonio. I knew only that I felt a liking for that little boy who was already so adult, already so much better than me.

Francesco waved at me through the window. With his hand he imitated a strange animal that was walking over the glass. Then I understood.

"Don't worry," I said. "I'll look after the ants."

The train pulled away. I remained there for a few minutes, fixed to the empty platform. I felt truly alone.

I SPENT FOUR MORE MONTHS AT THE HOUSE IN TORA, IN complete isolation. I had no calendar and soon lost count of the days. I could live on what I grew, and with my spare money I bought notebooks so that I could keep writing the monologue for what I imagined to be the new show.

I never wrote to Teresa, nor did she write to me, but every so often in my breast I felt a pang for her.

I hadn't been back to the place where we buried Nicolas. On my last day in Tora, I spent a few minutes by the tree that grew there beside him. The rains had leveled the ground. Everything had returned to its place. Sooner or later the roots would wrap themselves around what was left of Nicolas.

A NOTE FROM THE TRANSLATOR

This is a story about words, about their sound and how they are formed, about how they can become a weapon, a shield, a means of escape, a path to freedom, a path that leads to a larger and more complex world.

Davide is the only son of Tommaso Buonasorte, owner of fifteen pigs. The family name means "good fortune," and in the local village they say words contain the truth, or its opposite. Davide's life so far seems to offer little room for hope. He was born with a crippled right leg, and his illiterate father bans him from going to school—"One pig plus another pig makes two pigs, and once you know that you can work out the more difficult stuff." Davide's future is to keep pigs.

Living in a remote part of southern Italy, the family speaks a dialect that "connected our village's living and its dead," a dialect different from that of the next village, or from the next valley, or the one spoken fifty miles away in Naples. It is the language spoken before the days of radio, television, and the internet, when a standard Italian language was still in its infancy.

The first time Davide hears real Italian is when Nicolas and his father arrive with thirty Jewish internees from Naples just after the beginning of World War II. They speak "perfect Italian," a direct, precise language, "full of air, full of light," one that not even the local schoolteacher uses. Words spoken in "proper" Italian come out quite differently, "their sound and meaning are unified." *Maiali*, "pigs," becomes something new, and our narrator describes the fascination of hearing how "the *m* rests on the *a*, and that short *i* is a run-up to the last letters."

When Davide meets Teresa, he is instantly attracted and strives to speak "not in the language we spoke in the village, which seemed debased by the animals and the land." Instead, "I searched for words that would make a good impression." Language becomes a vehicle through which he hears about places beyond his own valley. She tells him about the Alps, about Pompeii and Herculaneum, about the Colosseum, the pyramids, the ocean, and the house on the Amalfi coast where she and her family would go each summer. She tells him about the man who used to visit her father's rope factory and taught her words of English like *dog*, *water*, *sky*, *yellow*.

Soon he is writing down all that he sees around him, filling pages of the notebooks he quietly steals from Don Aniello Panzer's truck on market day—words like *water*, *stone*, *bread*, *earth*, *nails*, *eat*, *death*, *father*, and that mysterious phrase he had heard Nicolas recite, "in the deep bosom of the ocean." He wants to write down the names he has given to his pigs: Grosso, Macchia, Cattivo, Nero. Davide is interested in the words themselves, beyond their sound. It doesn't matter here how they are written in Italian. It's the act of writing and the discovery of a new written language, an excitement that must be felt also by the reader.

When it comes to dialect, many words in this story will look strange even to the Italian reader, but while Italian readers are likely to have some inkling as to the meaning, English readers will be left at sea. There are no exact equivalents for many exotic expressions, so I must leave them in the original dialect and add a few words of explanation for each. "Most of the nicknames in the village came from the animal world: *cape 'e cuniglio*, rabbit head; *pier 'e gallin*, hen foot; *'o micione*, the tomcat." Likewise, the villagers called Davide by many names: "*sciancatu*, hop-along; *abbuccato*, crook-shank; or *guallaruso*, bandy-legs."

Some words of "proper" Italian also needed to be kept. Sometimes it's to preserve their sound, like the word *cianfrusaglie*, "junk . . . a word full of curves, of hidden indentations, ups and downs—like the village that went up from the archway to the tower." Elsewhere, there's a word that has more than one meaning, such as *glicine*, which, as well as being Teresa's surname, is also a flower and a color (wisteria).

When he arrives in Naples in the back of Don Aniello's truck, he finds himself a foreigner in a city that speaks another language: There's no chance of a job if you can't even speak Neapolitan. So Davide learns a new language. And yet, even then, "Each time I need to say something, I think it in our dialect, then translate into Italian or Neapolitan. The truth is that every thought I have passes first through these places, then ends up where I happen to be."

Readers may recognize the experience of cultural and linguistic assimilation, especially those who have moved away from their home roots. I, too, am a migrant, though out of choice. I have lived in Italy for thirty-five years, know the language well, and know the dialects of the towns and villages around where I live, and yet, however well I might speak my new tongue, it is transfused by the language and the ideas that I learned in the first years of my life.

Beyond this, the world has changed immeasurably. In Italy, there are people who still speak dialect, but everyone now knows the sound of "proper" Italian from the television screen in the corner of their living room, and cultural barriers that existed in the 1940s were soon eroded by the economic boom of the 1960s and 1970s that brought unprecedented levels of mobility, and depopulation of rural areas, particularly in southern Italy, as people moved to the industrial cities in search of work and a more comfortable way of life.

We translators depend more on our editors than we sometimes care to admit, so I would like to give my heartfelt thanks to Juan Milà, Alfredo Fee, and Judith Riotto for their invaluable support and advice, and to my husband, Peter Greene, whose critical eye over the past thirty years has saved me from more than a few embarrassments.

—Richard Dixon

Here ends Gianni Solla's
There Was a Time for Such a Word.

The first edition of this book was printed
and bound at LSC Communications
in Harrisonburg, Virginia, October 2025.

A NOTE ON THE TYPE

The text of this novel was set in Simoncini Garamond, a Garamond revival designed by Francesco Simoncini and Wilhelm Bilz. Released in 1958, this masterful revival was first commissioned when legendary publisher Giulio Einaudi invited Simoncini and Bilz to create a type for his new publishing house. The resulting type, loosely based on the original Garamond, found quick success and has since become a staple in Italian publishing.

HARPERVIA

An imprint dedicated to publishing international voices,
offering readers a chance to encounter other lives and other
points of view via the language of the imagination.